Bittersweet Pieces

Prose Series 13

Bittersweet Pieces

A Collection of Dutch Short Stories

Edited by Gerrit Bussink

Guernica

Montreal, 1991

The Editor would like to thank Julia Gualtieri for her editorial suggestions.

Antonio D'Alfonso, publisher and editor
Guernica Editions Inc.
P.O. Box 633, Station N.D.G.
Montreal (Quebec), Canada H4A 3R1

Legal Deposit — Fourth Quarter
Bibliothèque nationale du Québec
and National Library of Canada.

Canadian Cataloguing in Publication Data
Main entry under title:
Bittersweet pieces
(Prose series; 13)
Translated from the Dutch.
ISBN 0-920717-48-9
1. Short stories, Dutch. 2. Dutch fiction.
I. Bussink, Gerrit. II. Series.
PT5525.E8B48 1991 839.3'13'0108 C90-090253-1

Contents

Introduction

Bittersweet Pieces. Even if that did not actually apply to modern Dutch literature as a whole, it would certainly cover this selection of short stories from the last two decades of Dutch literature. The low-lying land, the constant battle against wind, water and ponderous skies and a centuries-old tradition of freethinking bourgeoisie, dominated by a Calvinist view of life at once strict and liberal — for the writer these form a well-spring for ironic descriptions and self-analysis. It is remarkable how Dutch writers wrestle with the contrary forces of liberalism and conservatism, conflict and pleasure, free thought and religiosity.

In *Moped at Sea* one of the characters drives a moped across the waters; in *Fear of the Roller Coaster* a woman shopper is subject to secret erotic desires; in *The Off-Peak Rail Pass* an innocent writer comes face to face with the bureaucracy which has wormed its way into all levels of society; and in *Indefinite Delay* a man gives an impressive description of how incredibly hard it is to get up in the morning. As this collection shows, Dutch writers are not just broody pessimists (although they can be), they dream, curse, make fun and philosophize. The Netherlands is situated not only geographically but also culturally between three dominant cultures. The wit of British, the theorizing of German and the aesthetic philosophy of French culture have, all three, had a profound influence. This could have resulted in an exaggerated degree of assimilation or in spiritual and artistic disorientation. But in fact it led to a completely individual position, only too grateful for the foreign influences it accepts and utilizes. What the effect on literature has been can be seen in this representative selection of Dutch stories.

Flemish literature, often considered to be a branch of Dutch literature, is not represented in this collection. This is because Flemish literature — even though the vast majority is published by Dutch publishing houses — has a character and a voice of its own, so much so that it would be better served by a separated collection rather than being subsumed under the literature of the northern part of the Low Countries.

The stories in the collection were originally selected for a radio project by Radio Netherlands, the Dutch International Service.

The translations were first presented before an audience by American actors in the Apple Corps Theatre in New York in 1989. The translations were adapted for the purpose by American radio producer Marjorie Van Halteren and myself, acting as Radio Netherlands' cultural editor. The recordings made in New York are available for broadcast by radio stations in other countries.

Gerrit Bussink

F.L. Bastet

Felix

She was just an ugly old lady living in a small apartment. Nevertheless, a lack of love had given her some odd traits which made her almost interesting. For years she had been a primary school teacher and dedicated to her work, she thought. But all those children seemed to have forgotten her completely. She never saw any of them. This gave her a certain satisfaction: most people were less virtuous than she.

After retiring, she lived a solitary life in an apartment on a dreary street in The Hague. It was called Obrechtstraat, after the composer, but the name was the only gentle note about it, and the people who live there are perhaps unaware of even that. Her loneliness was shared by a small cat which she loved. As much as possible, she kept herself hidden from the neighbours. She did the shopping she had to very early in the morning. She did not even know the people in the apartment below hers. To stop the people across the way from peering in, she had net curtains which she always kept closed. She considered herself quite a good person. Her only real sin was a sweet tooth — cakes, cheap chocolate — of which she was ashamed, but none of her neighbours would ever find out. With this she satisfied her wounded vanity. And since she had few surviving relatives, all the warmth she was capable of was directed towards the cat.

This animal was really remarkably small, a dwarf among cats. Even when it became aged, it still looked like a six-month-old kitten. That was not its only charm. It was also very affectionate, as well as intelligent and handsome: pale amber with a little brown, almost out of this world. Or so she thought. While she was not having an actual affair with her little Felix, her relationship with him was highly intimate, almost suspiciously so. Year after year, Felix calmly accepted her daily caresses, chatter, and other signs of love. He rewarded her by rubbing his head against her and meowing endearingly. Cats are sometimes extremely cunning in feigning affection.

Just as often, however, when it comes down to it, they reveal themselves to be essentially lacking in moral character. Almost to the point of behaving like sluts. Felix had been behaving oddly for several weeks. He would not eat. There were no more gentle meows. On occasion he uttered a scream that was nearly human. He drank without peeing. He was slightly swollen. Nothing could persuade him to leave his basket. One day he even had the nerve to lie down next to it, stone dead. Without the slightest warning. Three days before Mother's Day.

She was inconsolable and cried a great deal. Now there was no one left. She hoped she would not survive him for long!

But after that first day of intense mourning she caught herself lusting for food. She realized that it was scandalous and wrong. It seemed such a contradiction of her grief... still. After four treacle waffles, a piece of supermarket cake and innumerable lumps of cheese eaten with her fingers in the kitchen, she had to admit that her tears were over. Instead, she was overcome by something like anger. Felix had deserted her. It was almost a betrayal, of her love, her tender care. At that point, she knew that this death had hurt but not broken her.

And, furthermore, she realized that she was going to have to do something about the body.

Of course a decent burial would be the best thing. But she happened to live in an upstairs apartment with no garden. And as for asking the people downstairs... it was no use going to them — the corpse of a cat among their sterile flower beds!

A grey rubbish bag at the pavement curb filled her with aversion. Felix did not deserve that. Cremate him in the fire? She shuddered. She could have him removed by a vet or take him to an animal home. But what would they do with him? She was certain they would just take the remains to the dump.

Gradually she arrived at an entirely humane and acceptable solution. She would put him in a box and then "forget" it when she got off the tram. Felix might well have an all-day funeral following a route without end. Someone would eventually find him and bury him lovingly in his garden. That's what she hoped.

Deep in her heart she knew that this was wishful thinking, based on cowardice and self-deception, but she stilled her conscience because she also thought this would really be the nicest way. To leave Felix behind on a back seat, curled up in cardboard. To get off and never know where he ended up. She nodded, congratulating herself on being smart enough to think of it. She chose a nice big cake box, plain white, naturally. Any printing on it would have been in poor taste. A white funeral. She tucked soft cotton wool into the box to make a bed. It was regal. From long ago, she remembered the funeral of Prince Hendrik. Death was white, snow, a shroud. She closed the white box with a strip of transparent Scotch tape. Holding it out in front of her, she walked to the stop for the No. 11 tram, going to Scheveningen. Inside the tram, she went straight to the seat at the back and carefully put the box down beside her. It was spring, a fine day, late in the morning. The tram was full of sun. Most of the passengers were not going to the end of the line and got off earlier. With a feeling of peace and quiet resignation in her soul she reached the last stop.

She got out, leaving the box behind. Now her heart started thumping, because this was the moment of parting. She bravely swallowed the beginnings of a sob, and walked on stiffly but resolutely towards the promenade.

"Miss! Miss!" she heard someone calling behind her. She looked back. The smiling young tram driver was chasing after her: "Your cake. You forgot your cake."

Trembling slightly she accepted the box, muttered her thanks, and watched the tram setting off back towards the city. Now what? After long reflection she decided to go back to The Hague and try again there. This time she would be smarter. She would stay on the tram as far as the Hollands Spoor and then slip into the railway station. Among all those people...

As the tram reached the square in front of the station she was pleased to see that it was indeed very crowded. She got off quickly. She almost tripped over the tram rails and then the edge of the pavement as she headed for the station entrance.

"Excuse me, you left your cake in the tram."

A man in a corduroy suit held the box out to her.

"Oh," she said, with a sick smile, "thank you very much. How kind of you." She could feel — for the first time in how long? — a crimson blush rising to her neck. To recover her composure she went up to the ticket window.

The man followed her and said, "Could you spare me a guilder or two?" He held out his hand shamelessly.

Now this on top of everything else, she thought. Some heroin addict. One of those punk people. She put the box down by the ticket window and dug a coin out of her handbag.

Confused and at her wits' end, she bought a return ticket to Leiden in desperation. At least, it was not far. She had to go somewhere, after all. She looked so odd standing there by the ticket window. People were looking at her.

In the train, with the box in the luggage rack this time, she devised a new plan. She would get off in Leiden, but not until the very last moment, as the doors were about to close. It would take a very smart fellow to come after her with the box then.

She was absolutely determined now. At Leiden she stood up quite normally, only to waste time wrestling awkwardly with her coat. Then she walked leisurely towards the doors. They were about to close. Now was the moment to get off. But just at the last second a girl in jeans carrying a large bag jumped on as the train was pulling out. The girl collided with her and she nearly fell over. She just managed to grab hold of a handle.

"Sorry," said the girl. "That was a close call. Not hurt, are you?"

She straightened her coat and shook her head angrily. Ill-mannered child! And now, oh heavens, she was on her way to Haarlem. Without a ticket.

What now? I'll walk down to the buffet car, she thought. Then at least I'll be rid of the damned box.

So she entered the next car, where the girl was sitting with the bag between her knees. She got a book out of it. Must be a student. The creature had lit a cigarette and said as she passed, "I am sorry. I was so late. You didn't want to get off, did you?"

She shook her head angrily so as not to give herself away and said gruffly, "Certainly not. I'm looking for the buffet car." "Oh, it's the other way. I happened to see it as I was running by."

She turned around and went back into the non-smoking car, with an involuntary glance at the white box which was still in the luggage rack. No one had touched it. A foreign worker near the window smiled beneath his woolly hat. He pointed upwards. "Ah, box, eh! Forgot nearly, eh!"

There was no point in going any further. She was stuck with the box and so she sat down under it. A door banged open. A cheerful voice called out: "Tickets, please." Deeply embarrassed, she had to confess to the man that she was travelling without a ticket. He looked doubtful. There was nothing to be done. She had to pay a fine. On top of everything. How the other passengers stared at her, thinking: "tight-fisted old bag, bet she thought she could get away with it." Trembling with nerves, she stared fixedly out of the window, as if the yellow and red of the daffodils and tulips in the bulb fields really riveted her attention.

In Haarlem it all happened again. She left the box in the luggage rack, someone came after her with it. She forgot it in a teashop, someone came after her with it. She bought a bunch of flowers and put it on the ground half under the stall, someone came after her with it.

She threw the flowers into a canal. For a moment she was actually on the point of chucking the box after them, but she managed to control herself because again people were giving her funny looks. She went back to the station with the tiny corpse, took a train to The Hague via Leiden again, got the No.11 tram for the third time and finally came home to the dreary Obrechtstraat distraught, exhausted, and practically in tears. By now, the box was covered with finger-marks and beginning to look rather strange. Although it was late in the afternoon she decided to have a quick cup of tea. Strong tea, a hot cup, was what she needed. It might make her feel better. It had been such a strange, nasty day! She dropped into her chair at last. She was utterly worn out. The tea tray was at her side. She poured herself a cup and slurped up the brew. Delicious, even if it was only a cheap brand that she had mixed with leaves left from the day before. Excellent! Very reviving. You could put your mind to work and order your thoughts. The white box lay on the table. What on earth was she to do with those ill-fated remains? Wouldn't they be beginning to smell by now? She gave the box a furtive look. Her ugly eyes suddenly filled once more. Bleak self-pity threatened to overcome her. All her life she had had to get used to deep, bitter loneliness. But had she ever really succeeded?

She swallowed and got hold of herself. She made a decision. Tonight, when darkness had fallen, she would set off with the box one last time. A few streets away there were dark doorways, and she would either leave it in one of them or under a parked car. She would not look at the number of the house or the car, no, she would make a quick getaway and find oblivion in a glass of cherry brandy. There was no other way.

All the same she already felt a muddled sense of guilt. Poor Felix! She thought: what must he look like after being dragged around so much? It's a good thing he doesn't know about it. The little dear. Always so affectionate and such a comfort when times were difficult. She also thought: if he had a soul — and who can say? — he will be aware in the hereafter of all I did for him today. It may not have done much good, but I did it for him, and with the best intentions.

She drained her cup. And at that moment she could think of no better consolation than to be with him once more. To see him one last time. She could not bear to leave the box closed until the evening.

She put it on her lap. She slid her teaspoon under the pieces of tape. With a deep sigh and a lump in her throat she lifted the lid.

It was at that moment that the miracle occurred. A new transfiguration took place. For the rest of her life she would remember this as the greatest of miracles. How had it happened, in her own hands, during her tragic exodus on that long, endlessly sad day?

Inside the white box lay an exquisite, cream-topped, amber-brown apricot tart. On a white marzipan oblong was written in elegant chocolate letters: *To Mother.*

Translated by John Rudge

J.M.A. Biesheuvel

Moped at Sea

Isaac had been standing on the afterdeck for hours. He was a nice enough kid, but a little strange. When he worked on board ship he longed for a job onshore and when working in an office he longed for the sea. Isaac could not stand the monotony of shore life and had no money for cruises. But when he was at sea — working as a run-of-the-mill crew member (bespectacled and therefore always a cabin boy, mess assistant or officer's valet, never a seaman — let alone helmsman, his greatest ambition), he was confronted with the crude blustering of the seaman, who played cards for keeps with their knives on the table. Isaac simply did not fit in. At sea he was even more of a misfit than in his jobs in the harbour, the factory, the office or the bottling plant. Yet it was at sea that he hoped to find true adventure.

When his work was done, Isaac could always be found on the afterdeck. Midnight had passed two hours ago, but Isaac stayed put. It was a moonlit night, all the major constellations of the southern sky could be seen clearly, as could the fierce white backwash from the ship's propeller. Anyone who has stood for hours on the afterdeck of a moving ship knows that in the dead of night, in broad daylight, come rain or fog, in the polar regions or the tropics, in grey, green or clear-blue water, a ship always sails on a white road, a sea-way stretching from the horizon to the props, a road invisible to a castaway crossing it only fifteen minutes after the ship has passed.

A warm, inviting breeze was blowing. If you looked hard — you could make out the horizon and, a bit near, the light of a crossing ship that would have been heading straight for Isaac, had he been on deck an hour earlier. But, as we shall see, our senses can deceive us. There are philosophers who assert that everything is illusion, and who is to say they are wrong? Isaac's ship was a tramp steamer, and he had never seen other ships at night. He thought about how long it would take until he was back home. He gazed at the witches, the bollards, the hawsers, the railing and the easy chair he had brought up to the afterdeck.

Then Isaac saw the light in the distance swerve abruptly. It seems to make a tight run on the water and was now coming straight for him. As the light steadily approached, Isaac decided this could hardly be a ship; not only was it bobbing far too much with the motion of the waves, but there was only a single light. A ship running with only a stern-light? Too dangerous.

When the extraordinary vehicle had come within two hundred fathoms of where Isaac was standing, he recognized it as a moped. Finally something strange and wonderful was happening to Isaac. What he saw before him defied the imagination. At first Isaac was afraid, but when it came right down to it he simply could not believe that a new prophet or Messiah would move across the face of the earth in quite this fashion. Even though the Christians claimed that Jesus had walked upon the water.

By now the moped was only about fifty feet away. Isaac shouted and waved wildly, but forgot in his excitement to lower the rope-ladder. The man on the moped, whose accent revealed him to be a countryman of Isaac's, called this to his attention. The man steered his motorbike towards the rope ladder with remarkable dexterity and utmost caution; he seized up the sheer wall of the ship's hull like a boxer in the ring, first a few explanatory jabs, weaving slightly from the waist, shuffling the feet and blocking with his arms. Suddenly, in one fluid motion, he sprang — moped and all — onto the ladder.

"Careful!" he said. "Careful."

The man wore badly steamed-up goggles and a cap with great jutting leather flaps to protect his eyes and ears from the salt spray. The moped was a standard machine, with no special attachments. Isaac helped the man lower the moped to the desk.

"Give me something to eat," the man said.

Isaac went to find food. Below deck, he noticed that the seamen, the ship's mates and the engine room crew had all gone to their berths. When he returned he asked the stranger: "What are you doing riding on the water?"

The man claimed he was out to set a record.

"But how can you ride on water?" Isaac asked in amazement.

"It's a matter of practice," the man explained. "I started by placing a pin on the water's surface. If you're very careful, the pin will float. I gradually increased the weight of the objects, over a long period of time. Naturally, I was working up to my moped; eventually I was able to take my first, shaky spin on the pond in the park. Now I'm riding around the world. I never go ashore, but I often ride up to ships to get something to eat. I prefer doing that in the middle of the night, when everyone's asleep. The first few times I approached ships in broad daylight, but it was too much for some people to take. First they began shouting that this was the most wonderful thing they'd ever seen in their entire lives; then they began babbling or went completely insane. I'm out to cover forty thousand kilometres by sea, but I don't mind putting in a few extra kilometres as long as I've circled the globe. I want to do something no one has ever been able to do before. That's always been my dream."

"Aren't you afraid of drowning?" Isaac asked.

"Not at all," the man replied. "It's all in the way you steer, plus careful acceleration and deceleration, of course. For example, never take a big wave too fast or the sides of your tires will get wet. Once that happens you can forget it."

"Yes, of course," said Isaac, gazing in awe at the man who was stuffing himself with food and drinking large quantities of milk and alcohol. When he had finished he asked Isaac for a bottle of iodine, which he said he needed.

An hour had passed by the time the man swung his moped back overboard again and hung it on the rope ladder. He said goodbye to Isaac, who asked to come along as a passenger for the rest of the trip.

"I could even show you the way; I've worked on lots of ships."

But the man burst out laughing.

"First of all, you'd have to practice for years," he said. "But if I really wanted to I could take you with me. I can steer well enough and I could pump up my tires far enough, but I don't feel like it. Why should I? I've been riding at sea for months; why should I suddenly take you along for the last week? What sense would that make? After all, I'm out to set a solo record. How could I explain to the people at the finish that you came along for the final stretch? I'd have to give it everything I've got just to keep the moped rolling with someone on the back. Besides, I've never practised with a passenger. You're liable to make all kinds

20

of unexpected moves. You have to skip lightly, dance as it were across the water."

The man went on: "Do you know anything about tightrope walking?"

Isaac, who was not quite sure what the man was driving at, admitted he did not.

"Well," the man said, "you've got to balance on the moped and keep your tires as close as possible to the top of the wave."

With this, he bid Isaac farewell and climbed down the ladder with his moped. Isaac wanted to adjust the rope-ladder, but the man began shouting again (this time very loudly): "Careful! Careful!"

When he had reached the bottom of the ladder, the man started the moped at full throttle and kept the wheels spinning just above the water's surface. Several times he gingerly touched the tires to the water and then, without warning, hopped onto the revved-up moped and sped off across the sea.

It was beginning to get light. Isaac was despondent. Within fifteen minutes the moped had disappeared over the horizon. He decided to turn in for an hour.

In the morning he told the radio operator what had happened during the night. The radio operator shrugged and, when Isaac insisted it was all true, he laughed. Within an hour the entire crew had heard that Isaac had seen a man riding across the water that night. They all laughed.

At the end of the day Isaac was very sleepy. But, before turning in, he walked to the afterdeck for a moment. The sun had gone down. It promised to be another lovely night, but a bit cloudier. Isaac automatically began scanning the horizon. The man on the moped was, of course, nowhere in sight.

Isaac felt close to tears. He did not fit in onshore, he did not fit in with the crew, he did not even fit in with the man on the moped. He gazed at the dangerous turbulence of the backwash and at the birds flying along behind the ship. It occurred to him that he was a lonely man, and slowly he realized that he always would be.

He lit a cigarette and began humming a hymn. He could barely hear his own voice. The wind had picked up, causing the ship's propeller to occasionally come free of the water, spinning wildly before pounding back into the sea. Isaac looked at one of the sea birds and wished he too could hover and perch at will. He wished he could fly behind ships or far off over the horizon. Without realizing it, he began imitating the movement of an albatross' wings in flight. The bo'sun happened to see him and snickered, for he could see that Isaac stood with both feet firmly on deck.

Translated by Sam Garrett

J. Bernlef

The Trees

The noise at the intersection — the dark, jerky acceleration of trucks at the traffic lights, drowned out only by the kids' nasty mopeds — appeared to get louder at each and every doorway. She put her shopping bag down on the empty table the neighbours used to put their plants on and looked through the stained glass stairwell window at the people on the traffic island below. She saw their mouths moving, a child with a knitted yellow cap held in its mother's arm, its wide open, pink mouth bawling away.

Her panting diminished. Slowly, she felt the tingling, cutting feeling subside in her chest. She lifted the brown bag onto the table. It was heavy. Two days' worth of shopping, Saturday and Sunday.

When she reached the top, she let the bag sag onto the top step, pulled the key out of her coat pocket and stuck it in the lock. Cars braked. The light had turned red. That's how it went. All day long. She closed the door behind her.

It was quieter in the hall. She saw herself pass by in the small round hat-rack mirror, without really giving it much thought. She was thinking about Manuel. Or rather, she thought his name. *Manuel.* *Ma-nu-el.* As she walked to the kitchen with her shopping bag, she repeated the name to herself. Manuel. Her husband. Manuel. Forty-five years her husband. Manuel. His tearful eyes, as if too tired or infected to look. Manuel. The way he looked in the purple striped pajamas, shuffling around quietly in his leather slippers. She hoisted the bag with a sigh of effort onto the stone counter.

How come one morning someone decides not to get dressed anymore? Could you call that a decision? She hung her coat on the hat-rack rubbing the painful marks the bag had made on the fingers of her right hand. With a sudden airy, quick gesture she looked in the mirror and adjusted her thin, grey hair and with both hands; it looked like the way she used to do it when she was still young and had brown hair with a sheen and thought of other things when she went down the stairs.

She stood in front of the cream-coloured living room door. Her hand was on the black doorknob but she just stood there. She listened and, apart from the sound of cars and the tramway, did not hear a thing. When had she last been afraid? The olive green apron did not really go with her black, shiny shoes. She went inside.

Her eyes found him at once, a trusty object in its right place in the room. He was sitting in the easy chair and was looking outside at the intersection, beyond the folds of the opened curtains. He did not look up when she came in, but she noticed he had heard her because his back had suddenly straightened in his pajama top and his long bony fingers had gripped the wooden armrests.

She sat opposite him, looking at the traffic with him for a few moments. It was Indian summer. People were out without jackets. And still they could not open the windows. She had tried it once, but the noise of the traffic had been so deafening they could not even hear each other talk. Not a word. A grin suddenly sprang up among the white and black stubble on his cheeks. She smiled back. "Nice view," he said, satisfied.

She nodded.

She got up, went to the kitchen and unpacked the groceries. Was everything getting heavier because of the packaging, or did it just seem that way? Through the kitchen window, she looked out upon the narrow crowns of a couple of trees: poplars. Here and there she could make out sections of a few white wooden balconies across the way. She put the endive and lettuce in the vegetable bin in the fridge, spread out a newspaper on the kitchen table and began peeling potatoes. She looked out the window. She listened.

He had gotten up but had not wanted to get dressed. She asked if maybe he was not feeling well. He had not answered her. Just stared at her with his swimming eyes. She made coffee at 10:30 and put his cup opposite hers on the kitchen table as always. She called his name, but he had not come. She went to the room. There he sat in front of the window, looking outside, just like now. "I've made coffee," she said. She went back and drank her coffee, waiting for him. Finally, he came, quietly, almost creeping, in a way to which she was unaccustomed and that made her frightened. A word came to mind, a word she had not used since her teens: *Scary*. She drank his coffee without a word. Again she asked him if he were ill. If there were something the matter.

His face took on an expression of amazement, like that of a child who is asked something as self-evident as his own name. That's when he said it. Or rather, it was a question.

The plopping of the potatoes in the pot of water between her black shoes sounded hard and metallic to her ears. She stared at the waxy, pale yellow tubers at the bottom of the pot. She had missed a few bruised spots. Yet she did not bend over to take the potatoes back out. She went on peeling without looking at her hands.

Now it had happened. That's what she had thought. Now it has happened. She had not figured it would be this sudden. That it would begin on a morning in September, with someone who no longer wanted to get dressed. Now it has happened, she thought. And then two other things; the doctor; my daughter. The doctor; her daughter. For the slightest of moments and scarcely noticeable, she shook her head. No, not that. Neither of them.

She could see Dorien's garishly made-up face, slick and colourful at the table, in the middle of the room. And all that yak, yak, yakking. That it was better for all of us. To be on the safe side. If something were to happen to them? She had just let her talk. And Manuel? He sat in front of the window, rubbing his hands, saying nothing. For a long time. Just like he was not listening. Dorien had called him *Pa*, not Papa like she used to. Then he stood up. All of a sudden. Holding on to the back of the chair with one hand, the other hand showing her the door.

"And now, get out," he had shrieked. "Get out. Who are you, anyway?"

Dorien had gone without putting up a fight, without saying anything back. Insulted.

When Dorien left the two of them in that room both looked a little foolish. He with his hand still on the back of the chair, she in front of the table, her hands fidgeting nervously among the empty coffee cups.

"Who are you, anyway?" he said again, but softer this time, more slowly.

She had not answered the question. Nor did it appear to be directed at her, either.

She folded the newspaper with the peels in it, got up and stepped on the pedal to open the enamel garbage can. She put the pot of potatoes on the stove, but she did not turn on the gas. It was still too early. She looked around. Then she sat down again. She looked at her hands, swollen around the knuckles, at the potato knife in her hand. Outside, the wail of an ambulance's siren resounded. The hospital was nearby. Lots of ambulances came by in the course of a day but she never stood still to watch them go by like many people on the street do.

She looked around the spotless kitchen, at the row of different sized pans in descending order on the board above the counter, the wooden spoons in the wooden rack next to it. She looked at the pot on the stove, at the striped dishrag on the plastic hook beside it. She sat in the kitchen and everything was impenetrable and small and still, even though there was always the sound of cars, motorbikes and the trolley, but she had nothing to do with that.

Then she did something she herself did not understand. And yet she did it all the same. It was strange. Maybe even scary. With all her might she pressed the tip of the potato knife through the plastic tablecloth into the wood. Then she let go of the handle and looked. The blade stayed upright in the kitchen table, wobbling briefly before it fell back onto the plastic. With her index finger she rubbed over the cut. *She* had done that, she. She put her hand to her forehead. Was it warm or was she? She stood up and opened the kitchen window. The poplars, of which she could only see the tops, rustled absently.

She could tell by the sound of his voice he had not been joking, like when he used to come home from the workshop at 5:30. Now it has happened, she'd thought. And: no, not my daughter; don't call the doctor. She had to keep something secret, but she did not quite know exactly what. It was awful and it had to do with his eyes, with his dull, swimming pupils that had looked at her when he had asked the question. Looked at her without recognizing her.

Every now and then she heard a voice, a word from one of the balconies. She looked at the row of chimneys, the haphazard maze of television antennas on the rooftops. She turned her gaze briefly to the piece of blue sky above. Then she turned around.

Why it was she was so afraid of what she saw, she did not understand. For what she saw was quite ordinary: the kitchen chair that had been painted white, moved slightly away from the table. The knife she used to peel potatoes. She had just been there, peeling. Two days' worth because it was Saturday today. Yet she was scared. Her hand sought and found a yellow plastic watering can on the windowsill and filled it under the kitchen faucet.

She stood in the kitchen with the plastic watering can. There were no plants to water here. They were in the living room. Then she did something that again she did not understand but which, for an instant, afforded her a profound pleasure. She emptied the watering can out the kitchen window. The water vanished from her view in a straight line from the yellow spout under the windowsill. She did not hear a thing. Maybe the water had fallen on the grass down there. Like rain, it occurred to her. She put the can back on the windowsill and looked at a couple of drops that had remained on the dishrack. They were still moving. Sparkling in the sun.

It was Indian summer. Outside people were walking around without jackets, traffic lights jumped back and forth from red to green. She looked at the rack with the wooden spoons. In one of the spoons was a round, ground down hole. She no longer used them. They just hung there. Abruptly, she put the chair back in place in front of the table, went to the stove and lit the gas. Her movements were rapid and decisive. She blew out the match and made to put it back in the box. Her hand holding the burnt out match hesitated.

She looked at the picture on the box. Swallow. *Swallow brand matches. From Sweden. Säkerhets tändstickor.* Safety matches. It drove Manuel up a wall when she put the burnt matches back into the box. It was after all, annoying, but it was a habit, something she was used to doing. She went to the garbage can, stepped on the pedal that opened the lid and dropped the matches on the curled potato peels. The match caught in the folds of a wide piece of peel. She took her foot off the pedal and stepped on it again right away. The match had vanished. Slid down to the bottom after the shock, no doubt. Under the potato peels maybe.

Was there anything under the peels? She thought about it. Then it came back to her: leftover spuds from the day before yesterday.

Now that the gas was burning and the potatoes began thumping against the edges of the pot, she felt better. And yet she did not sit down. She was tired, but she did not sit down.

Funny how quickly you get used to someone in pajamas. Perhaps because now it was evening.

She served the food and he came to the table. He lifted the lids of the pots and laughed.

"Umm, looks good," he said.

He sat with his back to the window. Outside there was a great deal of traffic. It was always like this at this time of day, while they were eating. He sat across from her but did not look at her. He gazed past her at the photos on the sideboard. It looked like he was thinking about something. Then she felt it had to be done. It had happened, but maybe all was not lost.

"Do you remember that morning when you cut your cheek shaving? That's how nervous you were."

She heard her own voice. How often had she told that anecdote about their wedding day before?

The man across the table looked at her. His jaws stopped chewing. His eyes turned dark and dull and suddenly, once more, all hope had vanished. Then he made to say something, but she spoke first.

"Oh, of course, she said. We know that story backwards and forwards."

The man nodded and resumed eating. She looked at his mouth, and how he stabbed the potatoes onto his fork, how they disappeared into his mouth.

Again all she thought about was his name. *Manuel.* Why hadn't she let him speak? He does not have to take an exam. He does not have to prove he has been married to me for forty-five years. He doesn't have to say when pictures have been taken or who they are. He doesn't have to do anything. She tried getting angry at herself, to find fault with herself, but something happened which she had to keep concealed and she didn't know if she would be able to.

As she cleared away the plates, she looked at the photos. Manuel in tuxedo on the steps of City Hall, and she with her bouquet, one step higher at the request of the photographer as she was shorter than her man. Dorien as a child. Her wedding picture less formal, without veil and her son-in-law simply in a dark suit with a carnation in his lapel. And that large framed one at the top. Manuel at the farewell party at the workshop, five years ago now.

With the plates in her hand she walked around the sideboard and looked at him, standing there among his colleagues. He in a fancy suit, they in overalls. There was hardly any difference between Manuel and the man next to him. They looked the same age, just as strong and just as healthy. Everyone was laughing. It had been a festive occasion. There had been genever and beer and sausages and cheese with pineapple on those little wooden toothpicks. And his

30

eyes. They were happy and looked sharply and with concentration into the lens, just like the eyes of the others. Content and concentrated. As though they had a goal.

Again, she stayed in the kitchen for a long time. By the time she had come back in with the coffee, it had started to get dark. September was a beautiful month but night came early. She put the coffee in front of him and turned on the television. She went to the window. Her hand vanished among the pleats of the heavy, dark brown drapes. Then she let go of them.

"Television," she said. "The program's beginning."

He nodded, got up and slid to the head of the table. That is where he always sat when there was television, at the head of the table. She had said *television* and he had gone to sit in his place. She herself sat at the long edge of the table. In a wooden bowl behind her lay her knitting.

It was a detective movie. She saw how tensely he watched it, his mouth now taut, now relaxed.

"Good, isn't it?" she said.

He nodded.

He liked this kind of movie. She looked up from her knitting every once in a while. When there was shooting. Or when the tires made those screeching sounds during the car chase you had to look. Just like outside.

It had already begun to get dark. He was sitting, watching television and yet she had not closed the drapes like she always did when it got dark out. She looked at the purple and green neon signs across the way, at the illuminated drugstore window display. Sometimes a beam of light shot across the walls of the houses on the other side of the street when a car came careening around the intersection with its brights on.

31

The movie came to an end in a flurry of violin music. She got up and put her knitting back in the bowl. It would be a children's jacket for Peter. When it was finished she would send it to Dorien in a package. Maybe with an accompanying letter. She brought the coffee cups to the kitchen. Through the open kitchen window she heard the same violin music coming from across the way. She put the cups on the counter and went back to the living room.

He had turned off the television and stood there in the room, so strangely like that time before. He was standing with his face turned to the sideboard to where the photographs looked like dark rectangles hanging against the wallpaper.

Was he looking at the photographs, was he trying to recall who he was in the semi-darkness?

She herself stood there with the doorknob in her hands. Neither inside nor out. She did not dare speak to him, standing there, rigid in the darkness. She did not even dare turn on the lights.

"Shall we go to bed?" she said.

"Yes, I'm tired," he replied, and that answer, those words sounded so deliciously normal to her ears, that she walked up to him and kissed him on his rough, hard cheek.

She heard him go to the john and put his dentures in a glass of water. She could imagine precisely how he stood there, slightly bent over in his pajamas, taking a quick peek in the bathroom mirror at those surprised wrinkles of his. She had seen it so often. She lay in bed waiting for him. Then in the hall she heard a hanger fall to the floor.

"Manuel," she cried. "Manuel, what are you doing?"

She got out of bed.

He was halfway down the stairs. He had put his coat on over his pajamas as he was walking, trying to button it up.

She stood at the top of the illuminated stairwell in her white flannel nightgown.

"What are you doing?" she said.

He looked at her in that strange way, his head perched on that bare skinny neck, tilted obliquely up at her. Like she was asking for directions.

"To the workshop."

"But it's Saturday." That is what she said as he walked further down the stairs.

She went into the kitchen and grabbed the white kitchen chair. She slid it under the window and sat down. "It is Saturday," she had said to him. It is Saturday. Not that he had not had to go to the workshop for the last five years, but: it is Saturday, as if he had forgotten that.

There was hardly any traffic now. Except for the odd car that braked, accelerated then vanished in the distance. Invisible poplars rustled in front of her in the night. She listened to them and just like the wheels of the train when she was a child, the trees now were repeating her name. Each time the wind went through the poplars, she heard her name. Who are you anyway?

The trees answered: "Anna. Anna."

Translated by Scott Rollins.

Bob den Uyl

The Hit Man

The grey sadness of Jonkheren Street is a thing you can touch. Hard to say what causes it. Just built in, I guess.

The street is paved with an undulating layer of cobblestones, the streetcar tracks undulate a little less enthusiastically. A dozen cafés, a couple of cheap eateries and fast food places and, for the rest, shops. You could call it a united shopfront, if you like. Always ripped up. Pipes and cables disappear quickly in the soft soil. It's the kind of street where a dirty drizzle loves to come down.

Sereyn stands at the bar of one of the cafés. He has just put his pistol in front of him on the dark wood and is looking at it. The décor of the place is meant to convey cheerfulness. It failed in the attempt; after all, everyone knows that people have to supply their own cheer. When it comes to drinking, any surroundings will do.

Sereyn is about fifty years old. He isn't in the mood for talking. You just don't put a loaded pistol on a bar without some form of explanation. He assumes the attitude of someone who is going to announce something. All eyes are on the gun — a strange apparition in our peaceful bar where there is usually no more than an occasional fist fight. A bluish, shiny pistol is something else again.

"I spent many years in the States," Sereyn begins nonchalantly. "I went there during the Depression.

Went on an emigrant boat, men with beards and lice, but it got you there."

He is silent for a moment and wonders why he had to produce that pistol. When you rummage around in your pocket and you feel that marvellous, heavy thing, then you just have to produce it so you can look at it again. That's only natural.

"There was a Depression in the States as well of course, that's where it came from. That meant bumming around, very little work, even less food. An adventurous life, sure, but I'm not interested in adventure. Fine, it seems there was only one way to make a decent living. Crime."

The man behind the bar fills his customers' glasses. He is annoyed. A man with a gun means trouble. However, he is quite right to assume that he can't change anything and resigns himself. "The States are bigger, so's the crime. Over here you've got a burglary once in a while or they beat up an old lady for a couple of hundred. It'll always be kiddie stuff compared with the set-up over there. I look around for a while, you keep on bumping into gangsters when you're looking for a job, they're into everything. I finally joined one of their organizations in New York. There are all kinds of possibilities in organizations like that. They pay you according to the risks you're willing to take. You can make a bundle as a hit man but you also have a good chance of being shot to pieces. So I became a hit man. Guys like me were hired out to gangs or to private individuals who wanted to get rid of somebody. Quite a varied job, with lots of time off."

The circle round the bar is very impressed. It's not every day they get to drink beer with a real killer. The bartender is upset about the fact that the telephone is some distance from where he is standing behind the bar. He hopes for the best and because he is so nervous he buys everyone a round on the house. The result is a more conspiratorial atmosphere, a few of them strike more gangster-like poses.

"I shot quite a few people in those days. Kind of reluctantly of course, but you put up with a lot for a pile of dough. Parties every day with broads and booze, as much as I wanted. You always get to a point when you've had enough, it gets on your nerves. That happened in 1939. I'd saved a hefty sum and one fine day I called a travel agent and booked for Holland. Not a soul could know about it because you just can't say over there: 'Hey, look guys, I'm through.' They don't like that, it's not very safe. I go to work and the next day, an hour before departure, I call a taxi and take off, without any luggage. No sooner am I settled here than the war breaks out. I worked for five years as a night security guard for a distribution office here, in the city. The war was a quiet time for me, I completely recovered from all that shooting in the States."

He indicates to the bartender that he wants another round. Some newcomers are quickly and quietly informed about what is going on and Sereyn senses that the erstwhile hostility has been replaced by understanding. It makes him feel good. It's not often that a hit man encounters understanding.

"The war is over and there I am. There's plenty of work, but not for marksmen. And that's why I went back to my old profession, I wanted to eliminate people for substantial compensation. It seemed to me that there should be a lot of demand for that sort of thing after the war. Then I came up against the problem that things are so much different here than in the States. Here you can't just go around shooting people because you're gonna get caught sooner or later, and that's not what it's all about. In the States you're backed up by an organization with money and

36

lawyers, and they make sure you got an alibi. The bosses plan a murder in every detail before you do anything. All you've got to do, so to speak, is pull the trigger and collect your fee. That's it, no hassle. Of course, the police know that you're a killer but they can't do anything. As long as you pay your taxes on time you're home free. The only danger is that you yourself might get shot by a hired gun, but I wasn't that important. How do you go about it here, in Holland?"

The audience considers the question. Sereyn feels that he is the centre of attention and looks around the circle the way a teacher surveys a class.

"The first part of my problem was: how to get clients without attracting too much attention. I came up with the following solution. I called up people who were in trouble because they'd made fortunes during the war and weren't very eager to tell the tax man where they got it from. I told them over the phone that for a certain amount of money I wouldn't mind getting rid of people for them. No one believed me, they'd slam the phone down or laugh at me. That's quite understandable because the concept was still completely alien to them over here. Until finally someone, who was in some real trouble, took me up on it and made an appointment for me to see him at home. I go over, he points out the man he wants to get rid of and we agree on a price, five grand. I collect half in advance, just like I did in the States. When I got home, I looked at the money and realized that something was wrong. After all, I could easily keep the money and just forget about the deal. The man couldn't do a thing about it. It's different in the States, if you renege on a deal there they simply hire somebody else to eliminate you. You make very certain that the victim really does get a bullet in his head.

Then you go to your client and collect the other half. You're paid promptly, no one ever thinks of holding out on you because they'd wind up the next morning in the gutter, full of holes. I just mean that everything fits like a glove there, nobody cheats anybody. It's different here. It was a big problem to me because I wanted to do my job properly. When I began to think about the other issue, how to stay away from the police, I realized that the solution was obvious.

From that moment on I collected half the fee in advance and did not commit the murder. Enough money on the table, and no police at the door."

The spectators made admiring hissing sounds, someone blurted out: "No kiddin'!" — it scared him so much that he ordered a new round.

"I knew that I'd feel like a crook if I kept all that money without doing something for it, so I followed my usual routine. I investigated the victim's habits and when I was well acquainted with them I made up my mind when I would make the hit. The victim walked down Duck Alley every day. No idea why, but that doesn't matter in my line of work. Duck Alley is narrow and dark toward the end. There are only warehouses there. I rent a car, choose a good spot and wait for the guy. He comes walking toward me, I roll the window down, aim my pistol and pull the trigger. Nothing happens because it ain't loaded. In that way I held up my end of the bargain, as far as I was concerned."

People nod their approval, they understand completely. Sereyn lights a cigarette.

"After I'd done that I began to wait. My client didn't know my address, everything had happened at his house. Yet he was smart enough to figure out where I lived. And one day he's standing there in front of my nose, bursting with questions and threats. I explained the problem to him, just the way it happened. He demanded his money back. I said that that would be impossible, I'd done all that work after all, and I had to live too. Of course I didn't demand the other half of the five grand, I had no right to that. He got very excited and began yelling about crooks and things. I grabbed my pistol and told him that this time it was very much loaded. He takes off and I never had any more problems with him."

Sereyn drinks with satisfaction.

"I planned to take it easy for a while with the money I'd earned and then go back into business again. Here's the strange thing. After a couple of weeks some guy comes up the stairs, introduces himself, mentions the name of my first client by way of introduction, and asks if I'd get rid of someone for him. I say: 'Yes of course' — but meanwhile I'm thinking that my first customer is trying to get even by having somebody else get fooled too. That's fine with me. I agree on five grand again, the man wants to pay me half right there but I say no, I'll call him. He leaves, I tail him, he really does go to the address he said was his home. The next day I kinda nose around and find out what sort of man he is and everything seems okay, at least he's not a cop. I call him and make an appointment. He shows up and puts twenty-five hundred in my hand. Then I'm busy as hell for a couple of weeks trying to decide when to pull off the murder. Again everything goes according to plan, I roll the window down, aim, and squeeze. Nothing happens. A little later my second client comes up the stairs foaming at the mouth. I go through the same spiel and he leaves. A month or so later somebody else comes climbing up my stairs with an assignment for a double murder. And after years of hard work I've built up a large clientele of disappointed people who can't go crying to the police and got to vent their rage on someone else. My address is at this moment an open secret in the better circles of society. Sometimes I even have to turn work down. Despite everything I'm not happy, I keep on thinking that it's not quite on the level. I don't like that empty pistol, I keep on pulling the trigger and nothing happens. It was different in the States, a great time, then you knew you were shooting, the bullets were whizzing all over the place. Here you only hear a click and that's that. I have to keep on doing it, I've got to make a living and put money aside for my old age. I am, you could say, modestly self-employed."

Sereyn sighs and the circle feels for him. He looks at his watch.

"It's almost time. If you gentlemen want to, you can watch how I carry out an assignment in a few moments. An old couple is going to pass by this café in the next five minutes. Both of them have to be gunned down, I think it's got something to do with an inheritance, and it wouldn't be the first time. You will notice that this is not a quiet street and that I am without a car. The reason for that is that over the years I've lost some interest, it's all fake anyway. Yet I keep it up, I keep the illusion going."

Sereyn picks up the gun, walks to the window, and pushes the curtains aside a little. The café is on a corner and standing in front of the window you can see all the way down Jonkheren Street. It's quiet and growing dark, the street lights will go on at any moment. The men at the bar slowly follow Sereyn and stand behind him in a half circle. Everybody wants to get a good look. In the tense silence they all look up and down the street. Sereyn blows his nose in a handkerchief that he holds in his left hand while he holds the gun in his right.

"It really is an unpleasant street," he says, "I don't know why. It always seems as if at any moment a thunderstorm is going to hit."

The people around him make no answer, they are on the lookout for the couple, everybody wants to be the first to see them. It is Sereyn who notices them first at the end of the street after they've crossed the bridge.

"There they are."

The tension mounts. They will be witnesses to a contract killing. Sereyn stays calm, the gun sits firmly in his hand. As he is wont to do at moments like this, he thinks back to the time in the States when he was a feared killer. Now look at him: in a Dutch café with the gin and beer breath of a dozen nervous regulars down his neck.

The moment has arrived, the aged couple have slowly made it to the café. Sereyn raises the gun, aims with his left eye closed, and squeezes the trigger. There's a click, he squeezes again, another click. Then he slips the weapon into his pocket and says without turning around: "That's it, gentlemen."

The spectators remain standing behind Sereyn a little while longer, they expected more than this. Time passes and nothing else happens. Sighing reluctantly they return one by one to the bar. The bartender gives them another round on the house. He is both deeply impressed and just as deeply relieved that it is over, that the gun is safely back in Sereyn's pocket. There was no need to call the police. After all, there's the liquor license to think of.

While everybody is raising their glasses, the bartender looks at the figure of Sereyn who remains by the window. He says: "Of course, it was fun to be part of this but, how can I put it, it was something of an anticlimax. He's a weirdo, if you ask me."

The men nod. They had fun, enjoyed themselves for half an hour, had a great time, but now that it's over the guy's history. Over by the window Sereyn looks down Jonkheren Street, his face becomes gloomier and gloomier, and the hand in his pocket is moist and trembles. He longs for the States.

Translated by E.M. Beekman

Hermine de Graaf

Eating Cherries

Yesterday I saw a maybug coming out of the ground. First, he carefully pushed his head through the sand and peered around, inspecting our garden after three years in the earth. Only then, his shield and wings became visible.

It happened at my feet. I didn't move an inch. The tin cans in the trees rattled against each other and the blue-silver aluminum foil rustled. For a moment, I thought it was my father, coming to relieve me from my watch over our cherry orchard. But it was only the scarecrow slowly falling down, with his jacket and hat still on.

I reached for my magazine, leafed through it, and listened to the birds ruthlessly attacking our cherries. The rifle was propped against the back of my chair. Lady, barking, came hobbling along. She has only three legs. The starlings and crows flew away. My mother also walks with difficulty. She has both legs still, but her hip is worn out. I heard her walking to the shed to bring the newborn kid-goat his bottle. She can't seem to get enough of that. Lady lay stretched out, whimpering. A fly was driving the stupid dog crazy. In the meantime, the starlings were back.

Next to our orchard one of the neighbours was busy seeding. He took a handful of seeds out of a large tray strapped around his waist and scattered them left and right. The horse's mane was shiny. Bored, he stamped his hoof on the ground. Seagulls, crows, and other scavenging birds came after the scattered seeds. In the orchard, nothing is safe.

I take my rifle and fire it three times at a tin can that swings back with a ricocheting sound. I have tied ropes to some of the branches and attached cans, so I can pull them up and down from my chair. Then the tin cans rattle and scare away the birds.

Three years ago the trees were sprayed for the last time. Each year the harvest is bigger, each year I have more cherries. My mother won't can them anymore, and the neighbours refuse to auction off our crates for us.

I used to dangle twin cherries from my ears when I still had awfully short hair. There is a picture, in colour, my mouth red from eating cherries, my blouse red from picking them. My father stands beside me, tall and tanned in a khaki shirt, his arm around my shoulder. I was twelve and we were good friends. The rifle alongside my chair is his. I lost my own.

Lady hobbles off barking. My mother must be nearby. I follow the circling gulls. She calls to me, asks if I want to go along to the orthopaedist. I walk towards her. She would like to see me with the same handicap, or better yet, in a wheelchair.

"If I leave, the birds will attack the trees!"

She shakes her head, irritated. "Why don't we go into town together?"

I have never liked going into town, she wants me out of the garden. Her black hair is turning grey and her skin has lost its suppleness. Her eyes are always moist, even when she's not sad. She wears Levi's and a denim jacket, trying to follow a fashion she will never catch up with. She does not dare go to the city alone.

I look at the ladder leaning against the tree and see a cat sitting on it. Slowly I walk away, feeling vulnerable with my back to her.

"Let those damn cherries rot," I hear her shouting. I nod, pick up my rifle, and open the latch. It's out of ammunition, I need to load it. Out of the corner of my eye I see someone move. I turn around and let the cartridge slide into the slot.

The scarecrow is standing up, his coat neatly straightened, the hat on his straw head. Our neighbour climbs on his cart to return home, the horse obediently pulling the wheels out of the clay. I shoot straight through the straw brain. What do I care about those damn cherries?

My mother starts up the Mini Cooper and drives up the dike, honking. I wave and climb over the dike, the rifle hanging over my shoulder. The wind is strong. The waves of the river slam the rowboat against the dock. A freighter with a Belgian flag sailed by a few minutes ago. I see a white dog and a woman hanging up the wash. Fortunately, my mother has taken Lady along. I have her to thank for the rash on my hands and on my face, too. She always licks me there. My mother says that's nonsense: animals are clean. Along the Ring dike it is quiet, only local traffic is allowed here. I sit on the dock. I like rivers, their sound and smell.

At one time the row boat was used a lot. Simon liked to fish with the radio on. He wouldn't pay attention to anything, not the float, not the water fleas, not the cows on the other side, not even me. He wanted me along for fun, but I didn't really count. At night we would go dancing in the village, especially Saturdays, because other days of the week he would rather play pool or chess, it didn't matter which. He let me watch but I had to keep my mouth shut, or when the bell rang, I could throw a guilder into the slot of the pool table, and then sit for another half hour.

He mostly talked about how good his thesis was. Six introductory pages had been approved but the rest was rejected every six months and couldn't get off the ground. My father was right: he was not, and would never be, a high achiever. He'd probably end up as a high school teacher. I thought that was rather contradictory, since he considered Simon a suitable boyfriend for me, and I am just as gifted as my father. Or at least, I could be his equal if I wanted.

Behind me a motorcycle rumbles. A man in a black leather outfit heads my way, stripping off his wool face mask. I don't want to know him. He has two leather gloves tucked under his arm, his helmet glitters in the sun and blinds me. I shade my eyes and cross the dike back to the orchard. The man follows. From my chair I pull the ropes and see that he is startled, but the starlings stay where they are.

"You have to move the motorcycle off the dike."

He nods and puts his helmet and gloves down on the grass. When he returns, he asks if we are going to drink tea upstairs. I shake my head. "My mother isn't here."

He stands there and says it's going to rain. I look up and clutch the rifle between my knees.

"You look healthier, Jelle. If you ask me, you've gained some weight."

"I eat when I'm hungry and not out of habit. You want to fatten me like a pig, like a dung beetle, a maybug."

Yesterday I saw one of those coming out of the ground, which is very unusual. It makes me sad. I look at the man, who has taken off his motorcycle outfit and is now recognizable as Simon's friend. He sits down on the grass. The gulls circle relentlessly over the trees, swoop down, circling and screeching.

"When is your mother coming?"

"If you want tea, go make some."

"These orchards aren't worth the trouble any more, they take too much work."

"This one has produced more than enough for me. The May cherries have never been so perfect — and no spraying!"

I yank on the ropes. He nods and stands up.

The neighbour passes by with his horse and cart, the Mini Cooper drives into our garden, and my mother slams the door shut. She insists on having tea either next to the house or upstairs.

I stop in the hay barn and look at the dusty shafts of light filtering through the rafters. Matthias and my mother walk up the stairs. She makes a turning motion with her behind: step... bump... step... bump... One leg seems slower than the other. I go to the apple bin, where it is cool. Before we came to live here, kilos of apples were stored in this room. Now it is my father's study. It smells like mildew, the Persian rug on the stone floor is faded. I nudge my foot against the kerosene stove which still contains some fuel. The wooden bookcases seem to resound. My father reads a lot. He used to read me stories but now I have to do it myself. Rows and rows of children's books — everything that belonged to him is also mine. My books ought to be arranged next to his study books.

I let my hand glide along the spines, but I take none of the children's books down. I know them all anyway, and my mother would call me "childish." She treats me like a child, anyhow. She's always bringing me sweets or pastry and tells people in the stores or on the street that I don't eat any more, that I throw up all my food! Probably she is complaining to Matthias this very moment, but he thinks I've gained weight. Poor Mother. I hear them walking to the garden beside the house, talking in muffled voices. Something falls, Lady barks.

I wait a minute and then walk into the orchard. Today I am going to pick the first May cherries. I tie the basket to my waist with a rope and climb the ladder. I see twin, triplet, and single cherries robbed of their fruity flesh, dangling on their stalks. The starlings fly overhead, the harvest is disappointing. Hastily I pick the cherries, pop a few in my mouth, and swallow the pits, as I used to. My mother always got mad when she noticed me swallowing them, but my father laughed and said a cherry tree would grow out of me. Only when I had tripled my cherry pit record did he get worried, and then held "pit-spitting" contests with me. I almost always won, spitting them from the dining room table against the window, sometimes leaving a small red spot.

Matthias is calling, but he can't possibly see me. Far away, he is a small figure who can only guess where I might be hiding. I climb down the ladder and go to the side garden. My mother is shelling beans, continuing as she looks up. A blue-grey film of melted lead floats on her tea. A cake with whipped cream lies untouched on a plate.

"That's perfect. I have May cherries."

Without being asked, I pull off their stems and arrange them row by row in the whipped cream on the cake. After that, I cut the cake and hand out plates to everyone.

"Let's see who gets the last cherry."

After one huge mouthful and another and another, my cake and cherries are all gone. I gasp for breath. They look at me in astonishment and say nothing. My mother's lower lip trembles. Matthias takes a bite.

"Watch out for the pits."

My mother tastes the cake, choosily.

"Delicious, Jelle. Cherrycake."

I cut her another large piece. Matthias can serve himself.

The sun hangs low on the horizon and a freighter passes by. A group of wild ducks flies overhead. A hawk hovers in the air, dead-still.

At night I can't sleep. I sleep badly because of the rash on my hands and face. People say you should eat for energy but I know the opposite is true. They eat themselves into a stupor, while I stay awake and full of energy. I didn't realize my strength until I decided to eat only when I am hungry.

The birch trees whisper in front of the bedroom, brushing their leaves against the glass. Gently I am rocked back and forth through the leaves... Then I fly to the orchard... No one is there yet, and no one will come. But no, I'm wrong... My father, tanned and pensive, is wearing the scarecrow's hat, except it's his own! I protest, but he doesn't understand me. He holds his hand over his crotch and slumps over. I come to him and sling my arm around his shoulder. Together we look down. Two stems hang from his groin, the cherries are red and crushed in his hand...

"Papa! Blood!"

My mother stands at my bed with a wet wash cloth and dabs my forehead. She has thrown back my blankets and is nervous. "Matthias was right after all, you needed to gain some weight. Look! You got your period again."

She is as proud as the mother of a twelve-year-old daughter could be. I am almost seventeen. She goes to the door to find a sanitary napkin in the bathroom. I get up immediately.

The moon hangs over the river, resting on a broad band of clouds. My mother makes coffee and says this kind of life isn't worth living. I find one more cherry pit on the kitchen counter and spit it against the window. She jumps up and before I know it she has slapped me hard, several times. She looks shocked and wants to apologize. I push her away.

We look over the water together. On the other side the cows stand motionless, sleeping.

"Matthias says you are nervous and underweight because you can't accept that what happened was an accident."

"What does Matthias have to do with me?"

"He thinks you should go away from here."

"That's what *you* think. You hide behind him, just as you used to hide behind Father. You can't fool me."

"Why can't you forgive your father?"

"I don't have to forgive him! I will never forgive him for wanting to hand me over to Simon. He explained to Simon how to deal with me, how to go about it. Did you know that he wrote the introduction to Simon's thesis?"

"Don't talk nonsense."

"I know it for sure. And besides, that was no accident."

My mother supports her head on the table with her elbows and stares at the cows. We sit still. The coffee is cold.

Ants crawl in the sugar bowl.

"The day before yesterday I saw a maybug coming out of the ground, which is very unusual. The larva must have been in the earth three whole years."

Her fingers touch my neck, and we look at each other. Her eyes are moist. Now she is sad. Maybe we see ourselves as we really are, dependent, unable to break away from Father.

She can't believe it, and right she is. For her, that was the moment when good must have suddenly turned into evil and evil into good. I get up and slide my chair neatly under the table.

Outside it is turning light, the starlings are lying in wait. I resume my post and give the ropes a tug. The rifle stands next to me. Soon the other cherries will ripen. It will be a busy time. I perform my father's duty and he performs the task for my conscience; without each other we are nothing.

It is earlier than I thought, too early for the birds. I can smell the river and, if I turn around, the earth. I walk from tree to tree and smoke a cigarette. I agree that this kind of life is not worth living.

Simon doesn't have a body any more, he has been under the ground for over three years. I have no remorse. I never even felt sorry about it. To me he never existed. I hear the first starling and aim; the shot rings through the morning air.

For my father, Simon exists day and night. He should never have forced him on me, it's his own fault. The starling flutters and drops straight down. His chest is bleeding. There he is, a meter away from me.

I must have loaded my rifle with a bullet meant for larger game. I could shoot down a cow, or Lady who is limping towards me. I grope in the pockets of the scarecrow's jacket, he and I are the same size. His pack of cigarettes is almost empty. Morning has broken now, and the sun glows red. Back then, I also must have loaded one of the rifles wrong. Didn't my father and I share everything? Simon wanted to surprise us — it was five thirty in the morning.

There is bird poop on his hat, and the bullets must still be lodged in his straw head. I pull him out of the ground and drag him to the middle of the garden. A scarecrow works best up high in a tree, not on the

ground. I drape aluminum foil all over him. The scare
of the neighbourhood: a murderer.

Translated by Johanna H. Prins
and Johanna W. Prins

J.A. Deelder

Dental Warfare

In the cruel winter of '44-'45, when much of Holland was suffering from hunger, cold and Nazi terror, and, thanks to the superhuman efforts of its staff *Crossword Puzzle* was still publishing every month, I was born. Rumours to the effect that I was sawn out of a fence at a construction site are true to the extent that, at 8.30 P.M. on the night of November 24th, 1944, in that Hunger Winter, *that* also happened. I'll never forget it. Outside: the Krauts, cooling their Teutonic rage over losing the war. Inside: the Dutch, shitting their pants by the light of carbide lamps or, if they had nothing to shit, as happened regularly in that Hunger Winter, sending their prayers on high to Almighty God, who, as was later determined, happened to be a collaborator too, and was therefore not susceptible. Cruel times, which did not neglect to leave their mark on those newly come into the world. An entire generation was scarred in this way, physically as well as mentally. A countless number of my contemporaries fell prey to rickets — the so-called English disease — complicated by calcium deficiency. In those days, humpbacks, chicken breasts and crooked legs of both the X and O types flourished mightily. In my case, calcium deficiency expressed itself in bad teeth. Not at first, of course, because you have no teeth when you are starting out but, as soon as my milk teeth began to appear, it was immediately evident that something was wrong — never mind how

53

wrong things would get later on. I can still see myself in my pajamas crying with a toothache in the middle of the night, fumbling and crawling up the stairs to the dentist rubbing his hands as he awaited me with a Satanic grin: "Come on up. Come on up!"

Behind me my father and mother, greeting the dentist as an ally, cut off any retreat. All I could do on my long ascent was scream: "No needle!... No needle!"

In later years, I managed to considerably transcend this particular fear of needles — in contrast to the way I dealt with my abhorrence of dentists, which assumed proportions which can only be described as epic.

A contributing factor here, if not the decisive factor, was the so-called school dentist. The one I had in primary school days conducted a true reign of terror. She was an old bag of 65 or so, who wore one pair of glasses over the other, and drilled into everything except the tooth needing treatment. Your tongue, your gums, the roof of your mouth... Nothing was safe from that bitch, whom I learned to loathe from the bottom of my heart. In connection with a national campaign to combat dental caries, she showed up every six months. As soon as I saw her assistant stalking the hall, heavily made-up and sporting the first of those plastic earrings, and shuffling through the peculiar peppermint stick-like cards that no one in the world would associate with a dentist, I was seized with an uncontrollable panic. I wanted to run, run away as far as possible from school and the school dentist, because you knew your turn was coming. And oh, that nasty bitch clobbered me every time. In my case, five or six cavities were nothing. She dealt with them all in one shot. I would return to class about five pounds heavier, teeth full of amalgam, or another one of those substances which, last year, they said were cancer-inducing (what they're saying this year I don't know because I haven't received the figures yet), but which were used very generously at that time. Fortunately, all those fillings eventually popped out, which shows how well that cunt had mastered her trade, but every six months, meanwhile, she worked me over good.

Some of my friends had a big cross on their dental cards. They didn't have to go to the school dentist. Oh how I begged and implored my mother to get a cross for my card too. But she stonewalled me. "Only dentist he'll ever go to," she must have thought, presumably not without reason, but failing to realize the sorry fate to which she had condemned me.

The path of pain.

They didn't use anaesthetics in those days. At least that old whore of a dentist didn't. All she said, as she drilled, was: "It's easy to see you haven't been through the war."

You were invariably dying from the pain. This was not only due to that dentist but the equipment she used. No pedal-operated drill, I admit, but not a whole lot better. Now and then, you could see the drill revolve with the naked eye. I've heard of cases where the drill stood still and the *chair* revolved. Ten revolutions and a drill like that was red-hot. That's when she branded your mouth again and again because, despite the two pairs of glasses, she did her executioner's work as blind as a bat. To cool things down she used the same water atomizer barbers used to slick your hair, and to top things off she had a kind of air pistol to blast away the last bits of debris.

Just think of it!

First the red-hot drill biting deeper and deeper into your jaw until it hits bottom... AAAAAAAAAAAH-

HHHHHHHHH!!!! Then, the nerve exposed, she squirts the water in...OOOOOOOOOOOOOOOOHHHHHHHH!! And for dessert, she gives you the compressed air treatment... OOOOOOOwwwwwwwwwwwwwwww!!!

I have endured much!

It was medieval torture you had to submit to every six months, for your own good.

(Recently perusing the 1936 *Dental Students'-Almanac*, published by the John Tomes Dental Students' Association, printed by the Printing Limited, formerly L.E. Bosch & Son Printing, in Utrecht — the things people do for a laugh! — I spied (between advertisements for stuff like *Wipla Dentures of V2A Steel, Meisinger Drills, Hand-made Ashe Extraction Pliers* and *Original Freienstein Injection Needles*) an ad placed by N.V. Almara, sole representative in Holland of the German Siemens company, in which precisely the same instrument of torture which drove me out of my skull in the 1950's was described as Siemens' *newest* of the newest, made in Germany around 1935, when the Nazi *Wirtschaftswunder* was making a deep impression everywhere and many a dental student, according to this same *Almanac*, would go on excursion to the east.

We went on an excursion to Berlin from April 22nd to the 27th, staying in the Hotel Central... Tuesday April 23rd. In the morning we visited the *Zahnärztliche Institut* where we were received by Professor Schröder, who gave an interesting account about making dentures. Dr. Rehm then lectured us on making casts and Dr. Kirsten told us about his special method for fashioning metal crowns. Finally, we visited the surgical department, which is under the direction of Professor Axhausen. In the afternoon we went to the Anatomical-Biological Institute and the showrooms of E.C. *Sanitas*. The first day finished with a guided tour of the city... Wednesday April 24th. We spent the entire morning at the *Rudolf Virchow Krankenhaus*, where Dr. Wassmund demonstrated several operations and showed us very many interesting patients. We took our midday meal in the *Harnackhaus* of the *Kaiser Wilhelm Gesellschaft zur Forderung der Wissenschaften*, where we were received by Frau Carrière-Bellardy. We visited the Anthropological Institute of Professor Doctor Eugen Fischer, where we were shown the famous skull collection and given an account of research into the characteristics common to twins... Thursday April 25th. In the morning a bus brought us, first, to the showrooms of the Siemens company, then to Siemensstadt, and finally to the Siemens Museum and iron foundry. Among those present at the lunch offered was Doctor Witt, a member of the Reichs-zahnärztenführung. We were then received in the *Zahnärztenhaus*, where Doctor Bunge addressed us about the work of the entire building and museum. The afternoon ended with tea at the *Reichzahnärztenführung* and a visit to the exhibition *Das Wunder des Lebens*... Friday April 26th. Professor Simon and his assistant Doctor Franzmayer gave a demonstration of making orthodontic pieces without a soldered seam. We then visited Unter den Linden University where we were welcomed by the Vice Chancellor and laid a wreath at the monument commemorating students killed in World War One. A bus brought us to the W. and H. factories, a subdivision of the *Deutsche Gold- und Silberscheide Anstalt*, where we were offered lunch and then visited the factory. Later on, Doctor Weski used patients to demonstrate and explain the treatment of periodontosis. The excursion ended with a communal dinner... We conclude this report with the hope that we can count on high participation in the January excursion to the I.G. Farben Factories, the Krupp Factories and the Vita dentures factory... *The Travel Committee.*

The result: hordes of dental collaborators in the war years. It wouldn't surprise me if, after the war, it was precisely *those* bastards who got the school dentist jobs.

My dental path of pain — further aggravated from the age of ten by wearing braces, which meant monthly visits to our own dentist who, although he didn't wear one pair of glasses over the other, stank to high heaven from bad breath — led directly to the decision that, as soon as I was on my own, I would never darken the doorway of a dentist's office again. I know for sure that I'm not the only one who thought that way.

I think that, thanks to the school dentist, my entire class foreswore dentistry forever. Some outcome for a campaign against dental caries!

No more dentists... I kept to that vow a very long time. The toothaches I got I treated myself, using any and all agents that existed for that purpose. By way of illustration, let's take toothache in its most acute form, when a nerve is exposed in a hole in the tooth.

In less serious instances, an absorbent cotton wad dabbed in alcohol can do wonders. But you should take care to use the right alcohol, the kind intended for internal use. It's 70 percent or 90 percent, I don't know which, but you'll find out pretty quick.

With toothaches of the middle or upper middle class type of pain (where a nerve is exposed in a hole in the tooth), try the ready-made toothache wads often sold in Chinese groceries. The active ingredient is clove oil. In primitive societies it is the clove itself which is placed into the aching tooth, and bitten down on.

When the problem is a really bad-assed mother of a toothache, the kind where you want to drive your head through a wall, then chop it off. All this to halt that nagging, uncompromising, piercing pain pulsating wave after wave of utter madness into your brain. That's when measures taken against toothache should get serious. In such cases — still talking of the instance of a nerve exposed in a hole in a tooth — I warmly recommend a wad of cotton drenched in Tabasco sauce. I guarantee that nerve won't bother you again for years. But you should be prepared to put up with the dark curls of smoke coming out of your mouth.

It could be, though, that there is *no* hole in the tooth, meaning the nerve is inaccessible, but you're screaming with pain anyway. What do you do then?

In such a case the tendency is to sniff, smoke, shoot up, pop and snort anything and everything which can bring relief. In this the danger of overdosing cannot be discounted; it could lead at worst to an early grave in which, with a probability bordering on certainty, one would be free of toothache for a long time — although, personally, I would not 100% rule out toothache after death. Consider that one of those five mummies preserved up in Friesland Province died hundreds of years ago as the result of an abscessed jaw — it doesn't take much imagination to see that this was a toothache which got way out of line — and, judging by the man's expression, he's *still* dying of pain. In the world of toothache, anything is possible. The only certainty is the toothache itself.

There are some toothaches that no herbal treatment can deal with. Toothaches which, no matter what you do for them, only get worse, and worse, and worse — finally becoming so unbearable that, in a burst of insanity, you go groping for the extraction pliers yourself. I'm not exaggerating either. The incident is straight from the annals of toothache combat.

What a person will go through in order to avoid visiting a dentist borders on the superhuman. But with good reason. The vow has been made: come what may, no dentist! It's no argument to say that any pain a dentist might inflict is nothing compared to the tortures you put up with when you stay away from one. No, fighting a toothache is something you do yourself. In the world of the toothache fighter, dentists do not exist.

Yet in the hellish world of the toothache itself, nothing is absolute, not even vows. A time came when I contracted the God-Almightiest mind-bender of a toothache I'd ever had in my toothache-fighting career. No matter what I did, it just got worse. The related cheek swelled to such a size that I had to support it with a hand to keep from losing my balance. I swallowed so much Saridon and related pills that in the end my heart was beating less than three times an hour. If I had to take a pee, the smoke rising from the bowl threatened to suffocate me. Pittsburgh, in comparison, was nothing.

And the pain.

It drove me nuts. Toward the end even suicide seemed worthwhile. Where do you turn to in a state of mind like that? To your mother, of course! It was her birthday and thus a pleasant surprise for dear old Mum. As I stood in the doorway, holding my cheek in my hand, she said: "What's the matter with *you?*" As if it wasn't obvious. I promptly burst into tears. The pain had knocked me silly. I felt I had no resistance left. I put my fate into my mother's hands. She immediately phoned her dentist and asked if he could help. *Her* dentist — because I had none. I hadn't been to a dentist in twenty years and, therefore, had no dental records. No problem. I could see him right away. And... I did. Not on my own initiative; I had none left. But because my mother sent me, just as in school dentist days. I didn't have to say anything to the man. He saw immediately how far gone I was. Even before I lay back in the chair, he had put four shots of anaesthetic into me. He yanked out three whoppers in a row, pus spurting to the ceiling. I'll never forget the face of the assistant, who'd been bent so studiously, clinically, over me. In one instant she collapsed — crash! — in a heap.

The dentist shook his head in bewilderment. "How could you let things go this far?" he said.

60

"It took a little work," I managed to mumble before, cheek still in hand, I stumbled out the door.

I was still flying from the anaesthetic as I headed for my mother's house. Halfway there, it hit me with full force. The unthinkable had happened! *I had been to a dentist!!!*

Not that it helped. In the years that followed, my teeth deteriorated further. Part of a tooth would break off, then another would chuck it in. It didn't cost me any sleep. As long as I had no toothache, I didn't give a shit. Every tooth in my mouth could chuck it in, as far as I was concerned. After that, there'd be nothing to worry about.

What about *after that*? What then? Dentures? This was truly a route I didn't want to travel. As long as the damage remained limited and nobody saw anything, I didn't need to visit any dentist. You had to let sleeping dogs lie. So, I used all means to maintain the uneasy status quo in my mouth. Until the day, quite unexpectedly, that one of my front teeth broke off. Even that didn't upset me. You had two of them, after all, I argued, and caries has to come out somewhere. Okay, I had a cemetery in my mouth. So what? I could live with a set of tombstones. I'd had bad teeth all my life. So fuck it! The more people advised me what to do with my teeth, the more I decided to simply let them be. Their condition grew worse and worse. Pieces of the root which had fallen by the wayside began to act up, asking for attention. At the slightest provocation, I awoke with a swollen jaw. I had abscesses by the dozen. A friendly doctor provided me with penicillin. I took hot baths to try to speed up the moment of rupture. Although you can grow a big mouth in less than an hour, it's at least a week before it shrinks enough so that you can be seen again in public. Since it only begins to shrink after the swelling

61

ruptures, the idea was to make it rupture fast. Reason enough for the boiling hot baths. Because they worked. Cultivate your own abscess and sit in a boiling hot bath and you'll see for yourself... In this way, I continued my personal war against toothache.

These were troubled times. The Tabasco bottle stood within hand's reach all the time. Overall dental overhaul came more and more into fashion. Crowns and bridges whistled past your ears. Friends and acquaintances defected in growing numbers. They could do any damned thing they liked, far as I was concerned, just so long as they didn't start bullshitting me about the allegedly humane methods of their various dentists. I just didn't want to know. Not only did dentists scare me shitless, I'd never be able to afford one as I was already too far gone and getting further gone by the minute.

There's an old saying that every childbirth costs you a tooth. In my case, it couldn't be truer because, the night before my daughter was born, toothache reared its ugly head once more, this time in the eyetooth next to the one which had broken off. Because there was no hole in it, I couldn't employ the Tabasco sauce. The hellish pain came from somewhere deep inside. Out with the bastard. *Radikale Beseitigung*, as Goebbels used to say. When I found a dentist to treat my tooth I learned why they call it an eyetooth. After giving me a more than generous fix, he got his extractor around it, gave it a pull and, then, after a quarter turn, pulled it out completely. At that moment, I very clearly felt something leave the corner of my eye. No wonder. The dentist showed me the tooth in question. The root was many times longer than the visible part. The tip of the iceberg. The end of the root became a vicious hook. So much for the quarter turn. I was glad to be rid of the bastard, although the hole it left plus the holes from earlier extractions began to add up to a — whatchamacallit — yawning cavern in my gums. Still, it would do, in my opinion. You can take a lot from yourself. Things couldn't get much worse!

The death blow came the day I sat eating a raisin bun with a slice of cheese inside — a big job for the one and a half teeth I had left — when — crack! — all of a sudden I bit on a baked-in pebble. That meant curtains for my second front tooth. When I looked in the mirror, I nearly pissed my pants. Gaping emptiness, relieved by two tiny stumps... It was more than even I could take. When I talked, I noticed certain sounds coming out as whistles or lisps. And I knew... this was it. Something had to be done!

After a long and painful inner struggle, I decided that the next time my partner visited her dentist, I would accompany her, for a purely informational consultation. Just looking couldn't hurt, after all, and perhaps a temporary crown for the half a tooth I had left would carry me through another year. As long as the worst gap would be closed...

But things turned out differently. Thanks to the dentist's energetic efforts, I am now the proud owner of a mouthful of handsome white teeth. Crowns, bridges, the works. I'd be lying if I said it hurt, the prick of the needle excepted. Because these days drilling under anaesthetic is the most ordinary thing in the world and dental equipment is nothing at all like the instruments of torture my school dentist used. Today, nobody with any intelligence would even sit down in that old chair of hers.

As I was made to understand that if I felt any pain I should stick up my hand, that's what I did... six times. And each time — bang! — another shot. By then, my head stretched from here to Madagascar!

Stoned out of my skull, I just lay back in the chair, comfortable under the bright lamp...

"Leave it to the experts for once," I thought to myself, letting that dentist have his way with me.

A great feeling of peace descended over me because, after forty years, I was rid of my fear of dentists and the war had finally come to an end.

Translated by Patrick McGivern with the author

Gerrit Krol

The Mobile Home

Where the city was expanding rapidly, on the south side, there was one mobile home left. It stood in the shade of two trees. These trees were removed, and dump trucks backed up to the site and filled in the ditches. Square lots were marked off, poles driven in, foundations laid, houses arose where cows had been grazing in the spring. Fall came. The new residents, in their large living-rooms, lit their oilstoves, looked out with their arms folded at "that old barrack," as they called it. With their boots on, they stood in their little yards, scattering grass seed and putting bulbs in the ground. Order came about. Strips of wire mesh, which were left lying around in the streets during the first few weeks, were removed by garbage men; a milkman made his rounds and a tree was planted near each draining-pit. In the morning the men went off to work with their briefcases and in the evening, when it was dark, they came home again. In the meantime the women, with an infant in their arms, with an infant in their bodies, or with no infant at all, looked out the windows and on the weekends their husbands joined them. It became a neighbourhood, with a soccer field and two goals. The mobile home remained where it was.

It was a kind of bus, with folding-doors and a footboard. The wheels had been removed. Saw-horses had been installed in their place to keep the body off the ground. The windows were blinded with black cardboard, except for the front window, which had real glass in it, above which — perhaps relating to the empty beer crates which were stacked up on the side, and at the back — red letters were painted: *Valhalla*. To the last *A* of this word a rope was attached, which stretched across the yard to the nearest streetlight, since its former support, an elderbush, had been cut down by the city builders. The inhabitants of the mobile home were rarely to be seen; it took several months before the residents of the new neighbourhood, however often they looked out of the window, were able to inform their parents on their Sunday visit, that "over there, in that bus" a woman was living with two men, brothers from the look of it, as far as they could make out by the streetlight, but only *one* woman. They called her Frija, just to give her a name. Where were they during the daytime? Sometimes, toward midnight, they could be observed doing something in their yard, calling out unintelligible words while cleaning out their bus. Then the woman would carry everything inside again on her belly and often one could hear the beating of a hammer, someone singing when it rained. The neighbourhood resounded with the noise of an accordion.

An article appeared in the newspaper, *We Want Sleep*, and beneath it the words: "Complaints from our new neighbourhood." In the following editions, letters to the editor headed *Mobile Home* were printed. These texts, numbered with Roman numerals, rapidly increased in number until the editor, as the paper said, called it quits. In the early spring a society was formed: The Society for the Interest of Meadowlark Street and Neighbourhood. From its regulations — which were delivered from door to door — one could discern the controlled indignation towards the mobile home, *Valhalla*, and its three inhabitants. They decided to wait until the summer.

Around Valhalla the city grew; three streets with the names of birds now bordered perdition. On the fourth side was a row of rosebushes behind which lay the soccerfield. This, too, was one of the grievances: the goal-kicking of the mobile homers, their violent goal-shots, and more and more often now that the weather was improving, a housewife, vacuuming her living-room, would see one of the criminals jump over the garden fence to retrieve the ball. She would tell her husband about this in the evening. "We will wait until the summer," he would say.

In the meantime the crocuses had come out and the daffodils, but in some of the gardens they had to start all over again: the city workers had been working on the sewage system and had exposed the bulbs, splitting them with their shovels; but the trees at the curb began to get leaves, all at once the soccerfield was green and one day the inhabitants of the mobile home showed that they had made something, too. They unscrewed one wall of their caravan, folding it down like the ramp of a ferry boat and pulled it out: a small vehicle, with the woman in it waving little flags. The two brothers walked back inside, came out again with large triangular boards which they attached to the vehicle horizontally with nails and a hammer: it turned out to be a little airplane. The woman jumped out, laughing, her hair spreading like a parachute. She pummelled the two men, who stood looking at their construction with their hands in their pockets, and ran up the ramp. The brothers followed her, pulled up the ramp and did not appear again that day.

The neighbourhood did not have to wonder for long. One Sunday the older brother, standing awkwardly outside the mobile home, spoke to some of the neighbourhood kids. It was the first time they saw him from up close and he allowed them to board the plane. "One by one," he said and in the meantime he took some snapshots. With a box camera he stood there, the sun behind him, snapping pictures and letting them take turns. It was Sunday, and their parents were standing at the window, two by two, saying "aha!" as if something had dawned on them. Many of them wrote letters to the editor that night. But a few days later, when Frija came to the door with the photographs and showed the mothers their childrens' laughing faces, those mothers were touched; they ran into the kitchens and into the living-rooms to get money. The Valhalla airplane became the neighbourhood attraction and on Sundays and on Wednesday afternoons children came and went, were photographed with or without a flying-cap, supplied their names and addresses to Frija, who sat on the grass with a notebook on her knees. The younger brother turned out to be the real builder; every day he arrived on his delivery bike with something new: a propeller, incomplete erector sets, and once even with a missile, for under the wings; was it a real one? And the grown-ups started to show some interest, too. They pointed out the technical details to one another, the simplicity of the construction or the complexity of it. A reporter from the local newspaper had wanted to submit the older brother to an interview, but he... "I dunno nothin'," he said and the bystanders burst into laughter. The younger one did not say anything at all. He was tinkering with wires on the tail end and Frija was hanging up the laundry. The bystanders laughed, but in the evening it was the other way around, then the mobile home laughed. Those who were lucky enough to live right across from the mobile home were able to look in through the front window, to observe the drinking and laughing and playing and fighting, whatever it was they did. A woman and two men, what exactly was going on they could not make out. "We have no illusions," said the chairman of the Interest Society. "We have no illusions about this situation."

Then Fall came. The airplane was almost finished. The passengers could make the propellers go around with a push of a button, stop them again, move the tail-fins, but the summer was over, it rained on Sundays and the number of children wanting their picture taken was so small that Frija with her two men preferred to stay inside, too. The rain beat down on the streets and one night, during a heavy storm, the mobile home Valhalla collapsed. It was in the papers the next day, with pictures and an article printed in bold letters. Frija gathered up the pieces in her undershirt; curtains and sheets had blown into the trees and the neighbours, behind their windows, thought: "This is the end."

It was. The next morning, Frija, with whatever she had been able to salvage, some beers and a box with some bread in it, boarded the plane. Both brothers had already taken their seats behind each other and she sat down in between. The propellers started to whirl, the plane began to move, made a turn, burst through the rosebushes, and there, on the soccer field, it accelerated with a roar, dancing and jumping. It lifted off the ground and, a moment later, was veering like a beetle, gliding into the clouds.

The neighbours left their posts at the window, it was done, it was all over. In the kitchen were a lot of dishes to be washed up, the children had to be put to bed and in the evening at seven or eight o'clock they turned on the radio, but they didn't hear what they had hoped to hear and neither did they hear anything during the next few days. No paper, no radio or television station reported their landing. Nobody ever heard of them again.

The remains of the mobile home were removed. The yard was dug up. A fence was installed around it. It was during the following spring that a truck pulled up. Men with tools jumped out with lumber and steel and on the spot where once the mobile home *Valhalla* had been they made a playground with see-saws, a climbing-cage, a sandbox and swings. There was a slide and a little airplane that was supposed to go up and down like a rocking-horse, but it was never used, perhaps from fear of it taking off one day. The fence was painted silver and they made an arched gateway in it with the letters *Valhalla*. In his opening speech, the Chairman of the Interest Society recalled the history of the curious threesome, as far as he could, because he did not really know much about them. Afterwards someone at his side handed him a pair of scissors and when he had barely cut the ribbon the children ran onto the new playground, pushing each other and stumbling.

Translated by Ria Leigh Loohuizen

Nicolaas Matsier

Indefinite Delay

As she switches off the alarm, can I hear it ringing *in reverse*? Once absorbed by the dreamer into his dream, even the briefest, most insignificant bedroom event appears complete with a history of its own, and so quickly that cause and effect seem to have changed places. Or was I just hearing the alarm ring the whole time? Sometimes the question only dawns on you a few minutes later.

Presumably, it was only the first of her rapid sequence of movements that actually woke me: she clicks the light on, climbs over me, starts the gas-fire hissing, switches on the radio. With the result (or am I asleep again?) that I can't hear her in the kitchen. Asleep or awake, I know every detail of these acts. They share a grim effectiveness: no thinking involved, sequence is everything, nothing is allowed to interfere.

I lie there; she walks — or rather stomps — around.

For a while the music, which neither of us is listening to, smooths away the difference between horizontal and vertical. Endless Albinoni, Boccherini, Corelli. The closed blinds still unite us. (Beyond them, cold, darkness, silence.) Inside, everything is filled in. There are no gaps. I am a participant in her actions. Nothing belies the impression that *I* will not be getting up as well.

But once she brushes her teeth, walks to the coat-stand and starts snapping bags, the distance widens. Now I need to know for if I'm asleep or not. Calling *Bye!*, she shuts the door behind her and goes down the stairs. I keep my eyes shut, thinking of nothing. I'm not conscious, that's for sure. But I'm not asleep: I'm not moving, that's all. My presence is as minimal as humanly possible.

He may have had things to do today, he may even have jotted them down last night, he may have asked her to remember to wake him up — I know nothing of all that. Totally blank, I merge into my own body, one which doesn't know if it is asleep, doesn't know if it can hear the alarm, doesn't know if it is comfortable or not. *For who is there to ask such questions?* My mind is the empiricists' *tabula rasa*. There is nothing to persuade me that I'm not asleep. So maybe I'm really after all.

I turn over. I've just turned over. I lift my head and look at the dial. Set the alarm for an hour later. Turn the hand twenty-three hours back, in other words. I'm awake, there is no denying it.

Having reset the alarm gives me a feeling of security, of legitimacy. I've convinced myself that I will be getting up in an hour. No problem. No problem, I say. Now I can suddenly remember having had things to do today (and jotting them down last night on a scrap of paper, which is lying on my desk) — but not what they were. Except for violent intruders, like the alarm, and hangers-on (and supporters) of my resolve to get up in a hour, like that scrap of paper, nothing springs to mind. And if nothing springs to mind, I am not here.

I press the right-hand button. Left for decision, right for postponement and repetition. Every ten minutes for an hour and a half, I will be reminded that I wanted to get up. The monotone is the droning memory of my will. The details of the postponement are left to the alarm-clock. Time after time, I can deny all connection between the buzzing and my will of the moment. And time after time, I can renew my old intention. But just as the buzzing will slowly fade, so there will be less and less will to be denied, and less and less denying to be done — for just as long as the clockworks of the alarm and will stay synchronised.

The classical music must have functioned as silence all this time, underscored by the velvet voices, *sotto voce*, intimate in timbre, naming names, dates, places. The words — *Koechel number... basso continuo... allegro maestoso* — smooth the sheets, tuck me in, straighten the pillows, and steal softly away without waking me up.

How many times have I switched off the alarm? The Remington Company assumes that the sleeper's finger, on its way in total darkness to the source of the buzzing, knows the difference not between left and right, but between ribbed and smooth. Whereas spatial concepts demand powers of abstraction, touch, the elder sense, seems able to get by without language. You need to be less awake to press the smooth button than to press the left one. Tactile contact is enough for the memory of touch. And so I've no idea of how often I've switched off the alarm. I didn't count. The memory is in my finger — which is, I admit, beginning to radiate a sort of physical *mood.* A mood that contains the exact number of times it has switched off the alarm. But it has no self-awareness. To put it more clearly, perhaps, I could say that I'm awake if the alarm isn't buzzing, and asleep if it is. Perhaps there's such a thing as a physical lie.

The voice that wakens me none too gently is a different class of voice: up-to-date, rough-and-ready. A voice that knows what's what. The voice of someone explaining, putting things simply. Right now he's trying to avoid using long words. What I hear in the distance is someone with a certain opinion of himself and his audience. I don't listen. I manage to live with it, like traffic noise. It was the surface form that woke me.

Is it getting lighter inside my eyelids? Once I'm not only awake, but also know it, I find it difficult to ignore the fact that the blinds are slanted so as to let light in the room. Daylight, which I know from experience does not so much complement the still-burning electric light as clash with it. What I am grudgingly forced to call my consciousness is now spreading throughout the house: I am no longer sleeping in the bedroom, but in a space slatted on both sides. In other words, there is no difference in effect between eyelids and blinds.

The act of listening assumes a quantitative difference between speaker and listener: you don't listen to yourself. If I find myself reading hieroglyphics in a dream, there's no difference between the text and my understanding, my understanding and myself, the whole dream being just an aspect of my sleep; likewise the school broadcasts — for seventh-graders — have myself as their cause. I read a newspaper report in my grown-up voice. After a short pause, I ask the question (in a friendly voice, as if I don't mind someone not knowing the answer): "Now then, what's a cabinet crisis?" We think about it.

First and second grade now. I am interviewing the stationmaster at Lage Zwaluwe. I answer the six-year-old pupil slowly and thoughtfully: "...I ring through, then I lower the barriers — we still do things by hand here."

A kindergarten program. "And what do you get from the baker's?" I shout: "Bread!" with the others. "Right. And a lot of other things too. And now, children, more about Clifford Cow and Percy Pig — you remember?" Mario sits there, nodding his head

74

really hard. "Anyway, Clifford Cow had gotten himself a telephone (do you remember?), and so there was that *bi-ig woo-oden* ear up on the roof, and Clifford sat listening for his Aunt Agatha to ring..."

Good grief. I can't stand it any more! *Shut up!* In one fell swoop I leap out of bed, run over to the radio, silence the voice, turn down the heater and put out the lights. I'm standing stock-still in the middle of the room, staring at the plants. It's hot — like a geriatric home in here. The only moving thing is the peacock feather, which the rising heat is jerking round and round in the neck of the bottle on the mantelpiece.

I know what I should do: pull up the blinds, water the plants, do what I said I'd do, sort out my notes, get the foundations inspected, put the washing away, finish reading the book, call her up.

And if I don't feel like doing that, I could leave the house, go for a cappuccino, take the train to Den Helder — because that's what it's called, or because it's the end of the line, or because I've never been there and have no reason to go there — see a matinée, go for a swim, sell a yard of books, hang around a street corner.

Then I'm in bed again, eyes wide open, overcome with utter revulsion. Apathy and rage in precise equilibrium, merging to give the taste of bad breath.

I've advanced the frontiers of unconsciousness, dozing and daydreams. I've turned over countless times. There's a limit to how long you can sleep. There's a limit to how long you can pretend to be asleep.

I dream I'm awake, I pretend I'm asleep. I rehearse the skill of infinite regression. I'm conscious of my consciousness, my disgust disgusts me. Each step takes me further away from myself.

I seem to be waiting. This chore or that, one plan or another, today or some other day — it's no longer the point. It's about getting up. But I need a reason.

The fact that I was just *walking about in the room*, with a concreteness putting even the most lucid train of thought to shame, is a riddle to me. There's no chance of me ever moving again.

I try to construct an argument to spirit me out of bed by force of pure logic. It seems incredible that a person can just think up a plan and then carry it out. It's as if I keep coming up against the same locked doors each time around. Where one train of thought would be more than enough, my thoughts become more and more diffuse. I don't know where I am. The question is, can the past become further away than it is right now — everywhere?

Was that a knock on the door?

The question answers itself with three more loud knocks in quick succession. I don't react, for this is no time to be in my pajamas. I realize, aghast, that the radio could still have been on. She disappears upstairs again.

I knew it was her all the time: by her knock, and because it's raining. Conversely, now I know it's raining (and has been raining all day), because she came and knocked on my door.

It's the leak again, of course.

From the moment she knocked, the restrictedness of my surroundings began to oppress me. Pretending I don't exist is no longer my own decision.

I want to get up, but mustn't make a noise. I want a light on, but it mustn't be visible. I want to leave the house, but with no other purpose than to return. Outside I dare say it'll be as dark as inside. I click the light on and grab a book at random — as if a light serves no other purpose than to read by, as if the

latter act is a logical consequence of the former —
and begin reading at breakneck speed, with the same
compulsiveness as I read a few paragraphs every
night before falling asleep. To avoid doing anything
else just yet. You only *know* you're awake in the
instant between waking and getting up, between
undressing and falling asleep — and I'm letting this
instant last, letting it expand to fill the whole day.

Functions are reassumed. I'll have to go to the
bathroom, it seems. I'm halfway out of bed before I
realize that flushing the tank will make too much
noise. As I read on I notice that I'm beginning to feel
hungry.

When I can't control my hunger any more, I get up
without a sound (just like that, from one moment to
the next), get dressed, and creep into the kitchen. I
can't put the light on — she might see it. In the dark I
fry myself some eggs and pour a glass of milk.
(Cardboard tearing, milk glugging, the crack of eg-
gshells, the sizzling of butter — what a racket!) I eat
by electric light in the bedroom: worn door-sills put
the rest of the house out of bounds. I have only
limited freedom of movement. That woman with her
blatant, four-square presence upstairs (now she's listening to records) is cramping and crippling my petty
actions. I chomp and read. Couldn't I just come home:
open the squeaky door carefully and then slam it
shut? I think of the pile of mail, magazines included,
which must be lying on the mat behind the door. I'll
have to wait until she feels like going out.

The records give me the exact measure of how
long she has been at home. This is the first time that
choice and volume don't get on my nerves. A few
times, for safety's sake, I turn off the light (unsure of

whether it can be seen from the passageway), only to switch it on again with the next record.

Although I have envisaged the possibility of the phone ringing and decided not to answer, I give in. I turn off the light.

With one arm outstretched to stop me bumping into things, I reach the phone. There's little sense opening my eyes. I give my name in a low voice. While I myself say as little as possible, I listen to a friend — who, completely at his ease, is *chatting*, for God's sake. I talk so quietly that he has to notice something's amiss. "Anything wrong?" he asks. "No." "Very suave," he says. While he's in the middle of an anecdote, I suddenly realize I don't hear music. A clink of keys. She's leaving! I hope, beg, pray that he'll keep talking until she's downstairs, that I won't have to say anything as she's passing the door. She clumps down the stairs. The usual speed, none too fast in other words. There's a lull in the conversation. He stops speaking. End of anecdote. Normally it would be my turn to say something. I don't speak either. I hardly dare breathe. Clump. Her heavy body has reached the landing.

"Hey," he says, "You still there?"

I don't say a word. She clumps along the landing. Now she's standing more or less next to me, with only the door separating us. I listen motionlessly.

"Hey, Nico! Is anything wrong?"

She doesn't knock again... She walks down the next flight of stairs...

"Nico! What's up? What's happening? Hello?"

I stay silent, in spite of the increasing urgency of the cries from the receiver, until the moment I finally hear the front door slam. I give some sort of explanation. We hang up. I head for the bathroom and listen with emotion to the roar of the tank. Then I switch on every light in the place: my desk-lamp, the spotlight for the plants and the one over the bookcase, the copper lamp on the coffee table, my reading-lamp, her desk-lamp, her reading-lamp, the light over the record deck, the one under the smoke hood and the one in the passage, to proclaim that I have returned. I put on a flute concerto. It's still raining, just as hard. I have a wash and a shave. I feel like a wound with the band-aid ripped off.

Translated by Francis R. Jones

Lévi Weemoedt

The Off-Peak
Rail Pass

For an inactive person like myself, I have travelled a lot, seen many so-called strange countries, and what a lot of people consider exotic regions. If this comes up in a conversation with acquaintances, I regularly note a kind of barely concealed envy and unstated admiration from the stay-at-homes. Who doesn't want to travel these days?

I am ashamed to say it but I don't.

My experience is that the two or three new impressions you get from a trip do not weigh well against the enormous number of headaches and feelings of emptiness and alienation that begin to engulf the traveller as soon as he gets underway. As to the strangeness of all those remote regions, the fact is that the entire world is beginning to look a lot like Amsterdam's international airport.

Things often go wrong for the traveller, too. Not that this is anything new. When Louis XVI left his palace at Versailles, in deepest secret on his first trip ever, the slow-motion fall of the guillotine had already begun. In a place called Varennes, he and the rest of the family were arrested and subjected to the crudest abuse. As the French historian Louis Madelin put it: "When Louis wiped sweat from his brow in the presence of the government officials, one of them said solemnly: 'That's what happens when you start travelling.'"

Right.

I could have written that myself.

I have travelled so far by bike, moped, car, bus, boat, Hovercraft, express train and airplane, but the only modern means of transport I would lovingly entrust myself to, without the onslaught of an anxiety attack, is the time machine. Best would be a one-way trip back to 1870. That strange country, those different surroundings, that is where I want to go. The rest, frankly, can't be scrapped quickly enough. But in the Netherlands of this day and age, I am still forced to use trains and buses. There's the Metro too, but I would rather wait till I am comfortably dead to be underground.

Trains and buses in this country are not very pleasant either. If you have to go somewhere and don't live in one of the four big Dutch cities, you are better off jumping inside an envelope and mailing yourself to your destination than hanging around waiting at a bus stop. If you want to get there faster, that is.

That's buses.

Trains are worse.

In almost any Dutch station around 11:20 P.M. or later anyone standing waiting for a reasonably fast train is going to be affronted. In the first place, the station will inevitably be dark, bleak and drafty. Secondly, a more careful look at the departures schedule may show a cross-hammers symbol alongside the time of the particular train you are waiting for. The crossed hammers have nothing to do with Communism, though, or with the furious labours of the railroad comrades in driving spikes and stoking the furnace or with boosting State production levels, or with wheels that are rolling for victory. On the contrary. The crossed hammers mean this train only runs on very special occasions — when Christmas and New Year's fall on the same day, for example. And the train that does show up an hour later, that is, at 12:32 P.M. only gets you to your stated domicile or temporary place of residence around the crack of dawn. That train is popularly compared to a dog on its nighttime walk, compelled to stop at every bush or tree and spray it with a thin stream of distemper, this to the increasing despair of its master.

And that's Dutch trains only from the outside. What are they like inside?

In the advertising of the Netherlands Railways or, to us, NS, everyone is always laughing in a Dutch train and the cars are an uncontrolled shambles of good cheer, with chickens fluttering about and mince pies sailing out the windows. I have to say, though, that I have seldom experienced such things. In actual practice I always pick up more sadness from my fellow-passengers than gaiety. Therefore, if I have to go somewhere, I always travel in the quietest hours when no trains are moving anywhere. I love little train stations when they are deserted but for the sun and the wind. I like trains themselves if they are confined to the Railway Museum. I have never felt the need, in other words, to cement a lasting relationship with NS.

Until something changed.

A day came when Netherlands Railway seemed to acquire some understanding about shy, retiring people and those who, through some defect of heredity or environment, do not want to chuckle loudly or belly-laugh their way through an entire train trip. NS began selling discount passes which made travelling in non-rush hours, the so-called off-peak, substantially cheaper. I had not thought a churlish, group-think, State-run organization capable of an affinity with melancholy and I was so surprised that I fell for it. I would have preferred a "depressed-hours" rail pass but you can't always have your way in this world so I settled for the off-peak pass. Even the name suggests an absence of warm human contact and conviviality.

So, one day I offered up to NS a payment of two hundred and eighty guilders. I received in return a transparent plastic case with an NS identity card inside along with the actual off-peak rail pass: a cardboard insert that had to be renewed year after year until the final end of one's journey. NS authority does not yet go beyond that point.

My wife got one too. Holding the passes over our hearts, we solemnly vowed never to travel the trains together, so as not to change the NS idea of what is off-peak.

Netherlands Railways did not give me much of a chance to break this vow. A month later, I was confronted by armed freight-shipping stooges who confiscated my pass.

At 9:10 P.M. on a Sunday night in March, I was sitting in a little bar-hop train that runs between the towns of Kampen and Zwolle — not a run, at first sight, with a potential for desperate events. But anything is possible in a train.

The conductor took my travel documents, studied them, and found that the numbers on pass and identity card differed by one digit; one said 3856 ED, the other 3857 ED. I took a look myself and could only praise the conductor's sharp eye, especially on the Lord's Day, when most Dutch people sink into a deep post-Christian era slumber.

But I wasn't particularly upset. I realized virtually immediately what had gone wrong, and assumed the conductor surmised the same. The wrong pass was in the wrong plastic case. I had my wife's, my wife had mine. Even so, it was all in the family and surely, after paying two hundred and eighty guilders, one was perhaps permitted a minor instance of neglect. Out of politeness, I confessed in detail to being clumsy, gave lively examples of similar mistakes I would make and promised to redress this one as soon as I got home.

That would not be till the next day, unfortunately, because business matters obliged me to spend the night in the town of Enschede.

Even as I was explaining things, the conductor had begun to write and just as I finished he tore a slip from his pad and handed it to me. Claim of the Netherlands Railways, it said. Train no. 8576, 2nd class. Cost of one-way trip: 17 guilders. Surcharge: 15 guilders. Fine: 25 guilders. Total: 57 guilders.

There were a lot of reasons why I did not fork over immediately, spontaneously, including the following: that very day I was travelling as a special guest of NS. As a brand-new steady customer, I had not only been sent two free all-day tickets but a friendly letter from the NS management, all this as *Wiedergutmachung*, war damages, for a recent wildcat strike in which conductors, like the one standing before me, had abandoned their duties and deserted their posts. It would be unfitting to fork over on a day as special as this; forking over would mar its festive spirit, be offensive to my NS host. I explained this to the conductor.

"Are you going to pay up or not?," he said.

I chose my words carefully, so as not to give further offense. "I don't think I will," I said.

At that, the conductor wrenched the off-peak rail pass from my bewildered grasp and stomped off in the direction of Zwolle.

I was no longer a non-rush hours traveller. In a certain primitive sense, I myself had vanished with the pass that now vanished behind the sliding door of the train car. On the I.D. card was a recent photo, and losing your shadow this way is very dangerous, often fatal. Even worse was that the plastic case contained two other snapshots: those of my wife and three-year-old son. I am a sentimental person. Just like truck drivers. I never travel without a representation of the little lady and the child in view. Think of us, it says underneath. The world is a cruel place, and this is a way to feel at home wherever I go.

I was so boiling mad at this ticket-punching clown who had marched off with all my happiness that I jumped up and began running after him through the train, sliding open the doors he had just let close. I was shouting nasty names, the friendliest one being Robot. Among other things, I likened the wearing of a conductor's hat to the owning of a pin-head and petty-minded brain. I was running many times faster than the little train itself but just when I was about to overtake my prey we reached the station at Zwolle. My frightened blue-clad rabbit slipped through the opening exit doors. He made a beeline before me for the office of the Railway Police.

By the time I stumbled in, panting, his self-confidence had been restored. Sticking out of the holster of the cop behind the counter was a reassuringly huge, pitch-black gun.

Speaking over their whispered exchanges, I told my story in a provocative way. In fifteen minutes, I had covered everything I could think of. My arguments had a degree of irrefutability convincing to anyone but a train conductor and an armed knight of Netherlands Railway. The credibility of my mistake. The possibility of verifying my story with phone calls to NS headquarters, to my wife, to my bank, if necessary. My papers, my good name and fame, my befuddled appearance. And also: how did I get hold of two free all-day tickets? And the senselessness of trying to perpetrate fraud using an off-peak rail pass with two different numbers. The warmly human NS advertisements: travelling hospitality, got the time? Cup of coffee, cup of tea. Railway pie. Innocent until proven guilty, at least off railroad premises.

But a hearing wasn't granted. Because, thanks to acquiring an off-peak rail pass, I had been railroaded down to the deepest valley of human stupidity. With my fellow travellers a blue-clad, pin-headed robot and a railroad cowboy with the understanding gaze of a Doberman Pinscher, whose only responses were: "Sure, anybody could say that" — and "People mess around with these passes all the time."

Like street cops, railroad cops are too dumb and cowardly to catch real thieves and swindlers, and always aim their frustrated weapons at the innocent. A few weeks ago, on a train in the neighbourhood of this very town of Zwolle, I had seen a horde of football hooligans — none with a valid ticket, never mind an off-peak rail pass — take the cars apart and terrorize their peace-loving fellow-passengers. The squadron of Railway Police, on board to maintain law and order, observed the proceedings from the safety of the dining car. As they explained for publication later on, this was a "withdrawal for tactical reasons, meant to prevent provocations of a more serious nature." I hardly recognized the train that I had boarded that morning, but the soccer animals got off in Zwolle cheerfully whistling, unarrested.

I, on the other hand, was here.

But I didn't fork over. Sunk as low as I was, I would test to its core the mettle of NS bureaucracy. In defence of that fifty-seven guilders, I was prepared to be drawn and quartered in the torture chambers of the Netherlands Railways.

I shut up, put on a grim expression and went and sat on a bench against the wall. Fifteen minutes passed. It was perhaps my surly intransigence which made my jailer begin to doubt himself. He started by giving me back my snapshots.

"Nice-looking boy," he said, leering at the picture of my wife.

When the conductor left, he slid a sheet of paper across the counter.

"You're in big trouble," he said.

Everything in writing. A copy of the summons, payable within five days. And my off-peak rail pass. I don't know which made me feel worse, but I picked up both and left the office. Tired and dazed, I looked up departures. It had meanwhile become crossed-hammer train time; the next train to Enschede was in forty-five minutes. Considering the late hour, the station restaurant was full. I drank the year-old coffee out of a cup marked with the hated NS symbol. I took the snapshots of my wife and son and put them back in the plastic case. Looking over my coffee cup, I saw two Railway cops come into the restaurant. Decked out in full battle dress, they took in the scene. The gleaming black leather uniforms made them look like they had come from the bottom of a nearby river. In this sinister attire, they made the rounds of the tables until they found what they were looking for.

Me.

"We have to confiscate your off-peak rail pass for the time being," said one, without much preface.

It was the public servant from whose company I had just escaped. All I recognized was his voice. The black leather made him three times bigger.

"Did they comb the entire station foot by foot before they came in?," I wondered. "Did they search under trains with flashlights, were they using dogs?"

My expression said: "Why?"

"Fork it over," the big cop said. "And make it snappy."

Before I knew what I was doing, I had given him the off-peak rail pass.

After the cops departed, I didn't look up when I left the restaurant. I didn't need to, to know that all eyes were watching me. And rightfully. I no longer felt as innocent as I had two hours earlier. Once you come into contact with black leather, it rubs off.

It was only in the train to Enschede that I recalled forgetting to ask for my snapshots back. My wife and child had been abducted. Halfway through these bitter thoughts the conductor came in. I had only my summons to show him and stuffed it into his hands without looking up.

"Real cute," said a voice above me, after the paper had been studied for some time. "I guess passenger control pays off."

My attitude must have reinforced his conviction. Because below him he saw a man ashamedly pressed against the car window, a perpetrator, a veritable sitting-guilty plea, with the beaten look of a dog.

Translated by Patrick McGivern.

Maarten 't Hart

Jaap Schaap

Usually I would catch sight of him as he parked his delivery bicycle across from our house. But otherwise I would hear him coming as, armed with a hessian bag, he went up to the first house in the street, where he would push back the flap on the letter-box and thrust his mouth into the opening. And then, not loudly but very penetratingly, so that his voice resounded right down the street, he would yell: "Oal-reh, oal-reh!"

Everyone sat bolt upright the moment they heard the sound of *Oal-reh, oal-reh!*; it would have been enough for Jaap Schaap to shout in just one letter-box, but he yelled into each one. There was nothing more exciting than to stand in the corridor and hear his footsteps approach. As soon as he had called out *Oal-reh, oal-reh!* at the neighbours', I would press my hands firmly against the letter-box so that he would be unable to open the flap when he wanted to call out. It took more courage to let him shout *Oal-reh* once and then to yell back as loudly as possible, making the mouth at the letter-box draw back suddenly. What I didn't dare do, but what the boy next door did, was to stick a piece of soap into the opened mouth after the first *Oal-reh* or to clip a clothespin onto his lip. In those cases the second *Oal-reh* — or, if you were very quick, even both *Oal-rehs* — would be left out, but he can't have been very surprised or shocked, for at the next letter-box you would hear him calling out again as though nothing had happened. He would always appropriate the clothespin as his just reward. Regrettably we could never see how he reacted to our pranks; we never dared to venture out or open the door when he appeared. What if he remembered that a clothespin had been stuck on his lip in the same street last time, too, and were to associate that with you? It is surprisingly difficult to convey the sound of *Oal-reh, oal-reh!* in writing, but even stranger is the fact that for years I did not know what it was he was trying to say, even though I knew perfectly well what the sound was intended to convey. It was his signal that he was willing to buy rags, cast-offs and waste-paper, in which he was certainly successful. Once he had completed his rounds through our neighbourhood streets, you could be sure of finding him, at the end of the morning, with his delivery bike full of old rags at the bottom of the dike near the sewage pumping station. Often we would already be waiting for him, a whole host of very small boys, ages four to six, and we would dash towards his bike, surrounding him till just his top half towered over us, and he would say: "Good for you, lend me a hand and give it a push."

Often there were so many of us that there was not even room behind the side-wheels of the delivery bike, at the tray or behind the rear-wheel and then you could only go up front to help pull there, and sometimes no matter how hard you tried you could not get a grip on it, so that you would just climb along, up the slope, with the rest of the bunch. Needless to say, we all pushed as far as we could, but the organization and coordination of the available force often left something to be desired so that Jaap Schaap often found himself hindered rather than helped by the gang of small boys. But he never got upset or tried to stop us, as he puffed and panted and perspired in his black jacket with the elbow patches. Sometimes he would raise his checked cap for a moment, and that was generally the signal for a break, halfway up the slope, when the delivery bike would be placed on the handbrake. Every once in a while, the bike would hurtle back down the slope, dragging boys along and scattering the rags as it went, so that if you hadn't let go in good time you would often still make a soft landing. But even when the bike did make the ascent safely there would still be boys who stumbled half-way, grazing or even cutting open their knees. They would run off howling down the slope, and it is my impression that some of the older boys used to give them a shove on purpose to make them fall over.

Once we had reached the top, Jaap Schaap would place the cycle on the handbrake and then would take the leather money bag from among the rags. He would carefully hang the bag over his shoulder, adjusting the strap until it was comfortable, and then, with infinitely slow fingers, open the fastener on the bag. We would stand around him in a circle, pressing forward, so that he would push back, saying: "Out of the way, out of the way."

The money-bag was opened, the left hand went down and re-emerged with a handful of small change, from which the right hand sorted out one-cent coins, which he would present to each of us. Very firmly he would press a cent into your palm, saying: "Here, a cent for helping push, take good care of it."

He said that every time, even if there were twenty children. They each got a cent, one by one, even those who had been unable to push because they had not managed to secure a place at the bike. Then the boys would scamper down the slope again with such haste and eagerness that often more knees were opened up, but at last the majority of them would end up in Mevrouw Kap's sweetshop, at the foot of the dike, where they would buy a bulls-eye, a piece of rock or a marshmallow with their cent.

Although I would have loved to go into Mevrouw Kap's shop, I always used to keep my cent. On Saturday evenings I would take it with me to Damplein square. At eight o'clock the members of the Salvation Army would appear, among them Jaap Schaap. I used to go along and watch on the Damplein as they stood there singing among the blaring brass, and above all I used to watch Jaap Schaap because I was firmly convinced that he not only could not keep in tune but moreover only muttered *Oal-reb, oal-reb* in time to the music. In any event he never gave a speech, although for that matter nor did any of the other male members of the group. They left the speaking to women — women in thrilling black nylons, who called for repentance in a particularly stirring manner. After the address a collection was always held, one of the collectors being Jaap Schaap. I would always position myself so that Jaap Schaap thrust his collection box under my nose. Into the box I would deposit my cent, thereby buying off the feeling of guilt that arose each time I had shouted *Oal-reb* at the top of my voice after he had placed his lips to our letter-box.

All the same it was curious that Jaap Schaap never gave a speech. Surely he would need at least some practice before venturing to preach at a funeral. For that, so I had understood from my father, was his aim in life. He had been present at every funeral for as long as people could remember, long before my father had become grave-digger. He wore his Salvation Army uniform to funerals and was often waiting at the entrance to the cemetery fifteen minutes before the burial was due to begin. He would tag onto the back of the sorrowful procession preceded by the bier bearing the coffin as soon as it set off at a signal from my father.

When my father first became a grave-digger it used to bother him considerably that there was someone else there in uniform apart from him. My father took a childish pride at being allowed to wear a uniform with a large cap at funerals, but the fact that there was someone else with a similar cap took the edge off his pleasure. But Jaap Schaap used to appear at every funeral, come rain or storm or biting frost. There were also many pensioners who used to go along to funerals, but they usually stayed away if the weather was bad. They probably came along because someone else's disappearance into a grave gave them a feeling of having escaped again; someone else's death forcibly confirms the fact of still being alive.

But that was not the reason why Jaap invariably attended funerals. Tired of the competition from the cap, my father had asked him one day: "Why do you always show up at funerals?"

Jaap Schaap had answered, "Look, you can never be sure that one day there might be no minister or anyone else to give the address. Well, if that should happen I'll be on hand to say a few uplifting words if the next of kin so desire."

"And that's why you hang around at each and every funeral in that ridiculous uniform?"

"Yes."

"Watch out for the stampede. Surely you can tell you haven't got a chance of ever being asked to say a few words."

"You never can tell. And just imagine if nobody was there, if the deceased just disappeared into the grave without a word being said about the life hereafter. The Big Boss would call me to account later: where were you, Jaap Schaap, when that old man died and nobody said a few words. No, that's never gonna happen."

Which was why Jaap Schaap attended every funeral, difficult though I found it to believe. Time after time I asked my father after there had been another funeral: "Was Jaap Schaap there?"

"Yes," came the invariable reply.

My father thought up stratagems to deter Jaap Schaap, but nothing worked. He treated him as rudely as he could, once, himself still in uniform, even knocking him over with a wheelbarrow he had hidden by the entrance. But Jaap Schaap didn't turn a hair. He knew how to look after himself; a clothespin on the lip is after all worse than a wheelbarrow in your behind.

Then my father changed tactics. He was nice to Jaap Schaap and matters even reached the point that, early one afternoon, he said to me: "Run along and find Jaap Schaap. There's a funeral this afternoon and he's sure not to know about it."

"Well, what's that matter? I thought the last thing you wanted was to have him there."

"Oh, he's a good fellah, why not let him come? He'd take it so hard if he found out that he had missed a funeral."

I made my way to Piet Heinstraat. At the end of the street were Jaap Schaap's house and storehouse. I could not find an ordinary door on the house, so I went across to the storehouse and opened the door there. I peered into a dusty gloom, in which, after a while, I was able to make out compressed bales of newspaper and rags. But there was no sign of Jaap Schaap, so I called out "*Volluk! Volluk!*" — which means, "Anybody home?" — but no one answered.

I ventured some way into the storehouse, plucked up all my courage and shouted, "*Oal-reh, oal-reh!*"

Still nobody stirred. I just heard a dusty cough, a failed echo of *Oal-reh.*

"*Oal-reh,*" I called out again, "*Oal-reh.*"

"What's that?" came a voice. Jaap Schaap stumbled through the storehouse, looked at me and then at my empty hands.

"Where are your old rags, then?"

At that moment I suddenly realized that *Oal-reh* was nothing other than a corruption of the words *old rags.* I stammered, "I haven't got any rags but my father asked me to let you know that there's a funeral this afternoon."

"There's no funeral this afternoon."

"Yes, there is, my father said so."

"Who's your father? Oh, yes, I can tell, the gravedigger."

"Yes, and he said that..."

"I don't get it at all. I didn't see anything in *The Link.* How can there be? And I didn't see anything at the parish office either, although I check there every day."

"That's what my father said."

"Well, I'll be there. What time's the funeral?"

"At half-past two."

That was the reason why Jaap Schaap waited in vain for an hour outside the cemetery. That evening, roaring with laughter, my father told us at the dinner table how splendidly Jaap Schaap had fallen for his trick and I bent in embarrassment over my plate for I, not knowing that my father was lying, had been a party to the ruse. I would not be able to buy that off with a cent at the Damplein on Saturday evening.

But it was as though this incident was meant to be compensated for, for at the next genuine funeral the thing for which Jaap Schaap had been waiting for twenty years happened. It rained heavily that afternoon; even the pensioners stayed away and there were no relatives at all because an old, totally solitary man was being given a pauper's burial. Only the undertaker and bearers were there. My father headed the procession and the only person behind the bier was Jaap Schaap.

"And what did he do?" my sister asked, when my father told us that evening.

"Well, he delivered a kind of sermon," said my father.

"What did he say?" I asked.

"He began by saying that the Great Rag Merchant up above had called a child home. 'Everything's transitory,' he said. 'You come up against it particularly in my profession. Day in day out you go from house to house to collect old rags and newspapers and then one day you've become an old rag yourself, a cast-off, and they stick you in a box. These days old rags fetch a good price but once you're dead they won't bid anything at all for you, except the Great Dealer up above because his son was hung on the cross like an old rag. Let us hope that He will be able to do something with this soul and that He doesn't have to take it to the dump.'"

"Was that all?" I asked.

"He said all sorts of other things about old rags and scrap-iron but I forget the details. He also led us in prayer and then gave a short reading from the Bible. But of course that's what he should have done to begin with. All the same he didn't make a bad job of it and I was glad he was there. It would have been a terrible thing if we'd had to put that man into the ground without saying a single word."

Translated by Jan W. Arriens

Vonne van der Meer

Fear of the Roller Coaster

When I walked into Casa Fantasia, a bell tinkled. I've never liked that. It's so compulsory, as if a lackey were pounding on a parquet floor with a staff and calling out your name in a booming voice. I would have to stay, even if I'd seen, at one glance, that there was nothing here for me to buy. Out of sheer courtesy, I'd let my hands wander through the racks and describe what I was looking for.

If there was one thing I did not want to do at that moment, it was to say why I had come. I would have been happiest just slinking around unseen. I was granted a reprieve. There was only one saleswoman and she was helping another customer. Neither woman allowed herself to be the least bit distracted by my presence. They didn't interrupt the conversation they were carrying on in whispers. They barely looked up from the boxes of tissue paper on the counter. They behaved just as I'd hoped they would: as though I weren't there.

Except for the whispering and the rustling of tissue paper, it was completely quiet in Casa Fantasia. I couldn't even hear my footsteps as I walked from the door to the rack in the middle of the shop. They were muffled by a thick, sand-coloured carpet which matched the pastel hues of the woodwork and curtains, and the filtered lamplight. In the mirrors — which looked as though they were covered with a thin layer of molasses — I seemed thinner, younger, farther away. They made me view myself more kindly, like a photograph from twenty years ago.

I spun the rack around. I felt excited but scared, just as I used to feel on the whirligig. This couldn't go on forever, because the haunted house was waiting, and the roller coaster.

Out of the corner of my eye, I saw him sitting there. In a room above the sales floor, behind a railing, sat the only factor which, all those times that I'd imagined how it would be in here, I'd never taken into consideration. The male factor.

The chrome of the rack turned wet under my hand. Let him be a sales representative, I thought, or the saleswoman's fiancé. Whoever he is, let him have enough insight into human nature to stay where he is!

I looked to see whether the other customer had already made her selection. If only she'd hurry up and pay, the saleswoman could take care of me. But no, a new stack of boxes was being placed on the counter.

I spun the rack around again. The thing to do now was to remain calm. Not to call attention to myself. Create the impression that I was a customer with the patience of a saint. And most of all, not to look at him. One glance, however fleeting, could be an incentive to him to stand, come down the stairs and walk over to me.

Try, I told myself, not to see him as a man. It's his job, he doesn't give it a second thought; he feels nothing. Countless times a day, he comes down those stairs. He does not see you as a woman at all. Think of him as a doctor. If a doctor says: "Would you please undress?" — you simply... But even then I blush, against my better judgment, and I am probably the only one left in the world who does.

"What can I do for you," asked the torso. It was wearing a shiny lavender shirt, with more buttons open than closed, had a chest full of hair and a gold chain around the neck. My eyes didn't dare go any higher.

"I'm just looking," I said. I snatched something off the rack, pretended to examine it and hung it back up. But the torso did not go away, nor did the rest of him. He placed his hand, signet-ringed, next to mine on the rack.

"Were you looking for something special?"

If only I could stare him straight in the eye and say it. If only it were something ordinary, like the title of a book that had slipped my mind, or a fishing rod.

"A nightie," I said, when he had repeated the question. It sounded respectable, like flannel, but he wasn't about to be fooled. Flannel did not make you blush.

"Something like this?" He took a flimsy black nightie from the rack, a spider's web of coarse synthetic lace. It would chafe harder than the most heavily bearded cheek, and as a finishing touch, a gold key dangled from one of the shoulder straps.

"Too short," I said, determined to reject whatever he showed me, even if it was the coveted nightie itself. I'd sooner have walked straight through the display window into the street than into a dressing room with his eyes on my back.

Better that than to have him ask through the curtain whether the size was right. Stick his hand through an opening in the curtain to take the nightie from me. Accept the money I would give him and touch my palm with his fingertips when giving me my change. And finally, hand me the package with words like: "Enjoy it." Unthinkable.

"I don't sell them any longer than this." There was disapproval in his voice: come on, don't be such a prude. "They're all this short, and I carry four different makes. Or perhaps you mean a babydoll?"

Before I could say no, he was reaching for a box.

"I sold one of these just this morning to another lady who was looking for a somewhat longer model."

He laid a black babydoll nightie, a kind of lampshade, on the counter, stroked the frills lovingly with the back of his hand and showed me the ribbons which held together or, if so desired — abracadabra! — no longer held together, the front and back. He looked at me questioningly.

No, the designer of this nightie had not been thinking of me, but of a young widow dancing on the grave of her newly buried husband.

"Not what I had in mind."

Once outside, I considered abandoning the whole idea. Was there one good reason to put myself through this again? Why didn't I go home?

But I couldn't get it out of my head. I wanted it, I had wanted it for a long time, and I knew exactly why. The sight of myself — the naked gooseflesh, the white skin on the white bed and always, summer or winter, mosquito bites — had become unbearable to me. Whatever anyone said or did, I could not believe I was still desirable. I would think, with each flattering word: "This isn't about me." With each touch: "Deceit." If he closed his eyes I'd think he was doing so to conjure up the image of another woman.

The woman who wore the nightie, the black silk nightie, was an uncomplicated woman. If this woman saw a roller coaster, she didn't stand looking from a distance, she didn't need hours of persuasion. She got on at once. With no effort at all, she forgot the bed, the living room, the house. She wanted to lose herself. She wanted to swoop and swirl, to be hurled through the air with such speed that she became a mere speck.

I'd been dreaming of the nightie the way an actor dreams about a prop. A walking stick, for instance, made of black ebony with a silver elephant's head for a handle. If he doesn't find one he will not be able to play his role.

I couldn't get it out of my head, rip it up like a note you're too ashamed of. The shreds would find each other again, become a single page that hovered before my eyes at night.

The lingerie section of the department store was in the farthest corner of the top floor. A trap. If you wandered around here you weren't scared off by the glances of passersby on their way to other departments, but you also couldn't pretend you were just another passerby.

I felt at ease here. Saleswomen — no men with hair on their chests — who seemed to have been hired for one reason only: their ability to express, with their entire beings, a lack of interest in the customer. Rummaging through the racks I felt the same excitement stealing over me that I remembered from long ago, when we had emptied out the dress-up chest: the moment right before pulling on and pinning up, when the choice of whom to become had not yet been made.

My embarrassment disappeared, but was soon replaced by embarrrassment of another sort. What looked charming on the hangers looked laughable on me. Words like lewd, foolish and cream puff came to my mind when I saw myself. Ludicrous, that's how I felt, not seductive.

I squinted hard and tried to see myself through different eyes, somewhere else, at some other time of day. But whatever pose I assumed, I did not for one moment believe in the woman I saw in the mirror. She stood there as if she had been squeezed into a costume against her will.

Wouldn't it be better if I just gave up? Wasn't it about time I admitted that no nightie, however dazzlingly black and shiny, could conceal the fact that I was getting older, paler? And that my lust was waning? No, that wasn't true, it was not that simple. It was as though, having been invited to go to the beach, I could not remember how it felt to wade in the water, and all I could think of was that going to the beach takes time. But once I got there, I would regret that I hadn't come much sooner.

I wanted to be able to nod an eager yes again. Like a first time, with a stranger. What was I supposed to do with that notion? Go out in search of a man, a stranger, and then another one after that? No, the only possibility was for me to become somebody else from time to time. That's why I was here.

Suddenly I understood what I was doing wrong. I was trying on the nighties as if they were sweaters. Do I feel at ease in this one? — was my most important criterion. And that wasn't the point at all. The nightie did not have to suit me, or the image I had of myself. On the contrary.

I took the bull by the horns and chose the nightie that I considered the most beautiful on the hanger. It didn't look anything like what I'd had in mind. It was much longer, practically a gown, but that didn't matter.

Quickly, before anyone or anything could stop me, I brought it over to the cash register. I took my wallet out of my bag and the money out of my wallet (and couldn't stop myself from working out all the other things I could have done with that amount).

We approached the cash register at the same time. He, a young man of twenty or so,. with a spool of thread in his hand from the adjoining department, and I, with my nightie. He nodded and let me go first.

From that moment on, everything went as a matter of course. As if I had thought it up that way, like a fantasy. While I was handing the nightie over the counter to the cashier, I noticed that he was looking at me. With growing amazement he looked from me — a woman, mid-forties, in a nondescript white rain-coat — to the thin shoulder straps, the plunging back, the slits in the sides.

As for me, I did not become confused, or lower my eyes. I did not pretend that the nightie wasn't actually for myself, did not say: "It's a gift."

When the cashier gave me back the nightie in a box, I eagerly reached out my hands towards it and thanked her. Before I turned to walk away with it, I looked the man right in the eye and smiled proudly.

All the way down the escalator, I could feel his gaze. I knew that he had followed me, that he wasn't going to let me go. I didn't hurry, didn't try, as I usually did, to get to the bottom more quickly than the step I was standing on. I just stayed where I was. I wished that the escalator would lead nowhere. Like in a children's book where an elevator shoots right through the roof of a department store into the air. But then, the other way around, a journey downwards that lasted for days.

As I walked towards the exit I didn't need to look back to know for certain that he was still following me, would continue following me, out of the store and around the corner.

When the light turned red he would come and stand beside me. We would look at each another, nod, cross the street together and walk into the nearest hotel.

At the desk I was the one who spoke up: "A room for the rest of the afternoon, please," I said in a steady voice. (He looked away, subjecting to scrutiny the plastic plants in the lobby.) I paid the bill and signed the register.

I had to think of another name. Barbara or Sabrina, a round, brazen name. Not out of fear that my deed might have consequences, but because I finally had the chance to present myself the way I wanted to. With another name and another past. And nobody to point out to me that I was fantasizing. The nightie would go on, and the old me — that sum of facts, memories, ties and responsibilities — would come off.

Stronger, much stronger than the need to be unfaithful, was the desire to be unfaithful to myself. I wanted to invent a story whose end I did not yet know.

The light had just jumped from green to red and back to green again. Hordes of people had passed me twice. I stood there like a stone in a river. I would let the light jump one more time, because perhaps there had been some delay in paying for the spool of thread. Perhaps he had lost sight of me. I turned around and scanned the crowd on the sidewalk, between the department store and the traffic light. But the young man with the spool of thread was nowhere to be seen.

On the way home in the bus I kept picturing him lying in bed with a girl his own age. Laughing about a woman he had seen. She had forked out a hundred and eighty guilders for a piece of black cloth with splits and lace, one of those would-be seductive

104

numbers. But she wasn't at all the type. They would shake their heads. Imagine thinking you could buy lust, or arouse it, for a hundred and eighty guilders. As though the allure was in the nightie. And they would kiss each other with the certainty that their passion was pure and would never fade.

Translated by Stacey Knecht

Biographical Notes

F. L. BASTET was born in 1926. He studied literature and archaeology and was the first professor of
Archaeology at the University of Leiden. Later he
worked as curator in the National Museum of Antiq-
uities in Leiden. Apart from his academic works,
Bastet has published a large number of collections of
poetry and short stories. The tragi-comic tale, *Felix*,
was first published in 1986.

J. BERNLEF (pseudonym for H. J. Marsman,
b. 1937) is one of the most versatile writers in modern
Dutch literature. He made his prose and poetry
debuts in 1960 and received a prize as best new-
comer. He developed into an influential editor of
experimental literary magazines and has written essays on literature and jazz. He also wrote a number of
plays and is regarded as one of the leading experts on
and translators of Swedish literature. His 1984 novel
Hersenschimmen was awarded the prestigious AKO
literary prize for literature. This novel, which was
published in English as *Out of Mind* (David R.
Godine, Boston; Faber & Faber, London) is an impressive description of the rapid disintegration and de-

scent into senility of a retired civil servant. *Hersenschimmen* has been translated into many languages and adapted very successfully for stage and screen. Thematically *The Trees* is closely related to *Hersenschimmen* and was first published in 1974.

J.M.A. BIESHEUVEL (b. 1939) is one of the most productive and most admired storytellers in Dutch literature. This is partly due to his memorable live appearances in countless radio programmes, theatres and television shows reading from his own work in a striking sonorous voice. Biesheuvel's stories are marked by the amiable, ironic way in which he treats autobiographical and religious themes (like many prominent Dutch writers, he comes from a strict religious background). The splendid *Moped at Sea* in which one of the characters rides a moped across God's waters is one of the most famous examples. The authenticity of the story is doubtless strengthened by the fact that Biesheuval himself served as a sailor for some time. *Moped at Sea* was published in 1972.

JULES DEELDER (b. 1944) is both a writer and a performer. Much of his poetry and prose actually has its genesis in this double role. His theatre performances regularly attract full houses of young and old. Alleviated only by musical interludes, his words are rattled into the audience at machine-gun pace. Recurring themes in Deelder's work are the German occupation of the Netherlands, memories of the Fifties, drug abuse and his love for the stars of jazz, R'n'B and blues. A notable feature of his texts is a comic and often absurd combination of weighty and vulgar linguistic devices. *Dental Warfare*, published in 1988, is one of his best known collisions between street talk and formal language.

HERMINE DE GRAAF is one of Dutch literature's leading young women authors. She was born in 1951 and studied Dutch language and literature. Her first collection, which included *Eating Cherries*, was awarded the 1985 Geertjan Lubberhuizen prize for the best debut of 1984. In the meantime, she has published a number of collections of short stories and two novels.

MAARTEN 'T HART works as an ethologist at the University of Leiden. His numerous books are among the best selling works in the Dutch language region. Apart from novels and short stories (in which memories of his strict protestant upbringing are a constantly recurring theme), he is also known for his essays on international literature and music. Many of his books have been translated and appear in English under the name Martin Hart. He regards himself as a storyteller in the traditional sense: "As far as I'm concerned a writer should first of all have a story to tell. Experience has taught me that if you're gripped by something, the form will take care of itself." *Jaap Schaap (Jack Lamb)* was first published in 1977.

GERRIT KROL was born in 1934 and works as a computer specialist for an oil company. Previously, he spent many years working abroad (South America and Africa). Apart from a relatively small number of poems, he mainly publishes novels and short stories. He very much made his name with short opinion pieces in Dutch newspapers and magazines. One notable feature of his prose is that it is not purely descriptive but is packed with intriguing argument and discussion about human thinking and behaviour. He said somewhere about his writing: "What I would like to do is write a book... which only really begins to live once you've finished it." *Mobile Home* was first published in 1976.

NICOLAAS MATSIER (pseudonym for Tjit Reinsma, b. 1949) studied philosophy and classical languages and was for many years editor at De Bezige Bij, the Netherlands' most important literary publisher. Despite his fairly slim output, he is still considered one of the country's most important young authors. Apart from his fiction, Matsier is also known for his opinion columns in newspapers and magazines and as a translator of English literature. *Indefinite Delay* is the title story of a collection published in 1979.

VONNE VAN DER MEER (b. 1952) trained as a director at the Amsterdam Drama School. Since then she has worked successfully with a number of theater companies. She also wrote a number of plays. In 1985 Van der Meer published her first collection of stories which won the 1986 Geertjan Lubberhuizen prize for best debut. *Fear of the Roller Coaster* comes from that debut collection — intriguingly entitled *Het limonadegevoel en andere verhalen* (literally translated: The Lemonade Feeling and Other Stories). She has had two novels published since then. Talking about her writing, she says :"As I write I'm learning to understand my feelings. I'm not writing things out of my system but into it."

BOB DEN UYL was born in Rotterdam in 1930 and is one of the best known and most popular short story writers in modern Dutch literature. He is also an authority on and translator of modern English literature. His wry, humorous stories are one long litany of human actions and thinking put into perspective.

Many of Den Uyl's stories have an autobiographical background, often incorporating travel diaries. The sympathetic misfits populating Den Uyl's stories are immensely popular with the Dutch public. *The Hit Man*, an absurd story about a cool-headed killer who is not a killer at all, was first published in 1968.

LÉVI WEEMOEDT (pseudonym for Izak Jacobus van Wijk, b. 1948) spent many years teaching Dutch. He writes poems and stories which are extremely popular for their peevish irony and humor. His central characters (as in *The Off-Peak Rail Pass*, published in 1987) are often people unable to deal with the situations they land in; they trip from one banana-skin to another, but along the way the reader glimpses the tragedy of the circumstances the "victims" can do nothing about. The tone of Weemoedt's stories is perhaps illustrated by this comment on his writing: "I shall have to do it alone. I used to think: perhaps the Muse will be with me, but I'm afraid she's not. She's stood me up. The Muse and I are having a sort of extramarital affair... She's got plenty of boyfriends, the Muse. Well, if I were her, I wouldn't go paying daily visits to a complete nonentity in glasses either."